Humanity's Edge

By
Tamara Wilhite

BLUPHI'ER
PUBLISHING

Blu Phi'er Publishing
Shreveport, LA
www.bluphier.com

 Published by Blu Phi'er Publishing.
Editing done by Michael L. Bernoudy, Jr.
Interior illustration and cover artwork by Robert Holsonbake

Library of Congress Control Number: 2005933529
ISBN: 0-9772034-2-5

Printed in the U.S.A.
First edition, December 2005

Please take the opportunity to read the following books from Blu Phi'er Publishing:

Negro in Nam: My father's Tale
By Michael L. Bernoudy, Jr.

Also, be on the look out for the following titles from Blu Phi'er Publishing:

True to Self
By Tilisha Alexander

The Chronos Project: A Race Against Time
By Marc Anthony Rios

Tales of Love and Woe
By Lawrence Strickland

Stained Glass Window: Memoirs of a Cheater
By Michael L. Bernoudy, Jr.

ORDER BOOKS AT WWW.BLUPHIER.COM

CONTENTS

Humanity's Edge

EDITOR'S NOTES

We, as humans, are caught on this wild ride, which occurs in the space between life and death. The span of this ride varies from person to person. However, everyone goes through the ups and downs of this roller coaster we call existence.

Many areas cause conflict during this ride. Love, of course, is a theme, which has inspired many poets and authors. A Trojan could tell you that love can bring about the fall of an empire.

Diversity is another cause of conflict in this ride of ours. Whether it be the "Master Race" attempting to conqueror all humanity, or skin tone, or religion, we as a race, clash over diversity.

As we explore our differences, the question has to be asked, "What makes one human"? Is the sum of life experiences? Natural birth? What makes for a good human? What's a fair representative of the race? The smartest? The strongest? The kindest?

As we as a race draw towards the end of this ride, we can only pray that we made a good run of it, as we draw near the edge.

NEW BEGINNINGS

You can't repeat the past, even when you have a carbon copy.

NEW BEGINNINGS

Arista pointed out the sunset, telling Father the sun was especially pretty tonight.

"Arista, that isn't the Sun. Look it up." The computers had all of the answers in those days. Or, at least, all the answers Father did not have the time to give.

The computer answered: "*This is the Delta Pavonis system. This star is located 19.9 light-years away from Sol. Delta Pavonis is near the center of Constellation Pavo, the Peacock. Delta Pavonis is a yellow-orange star of type G5-8 V-IV. It is visible from Earth with the naked eye.*"

Sol, the sun that Earth circled around, was visible some summer nights low to the horizon. Father had pointed it out. Aden, their world, had a wide axial tilt. Aden went through extreme seasons as it tilted on its axis. Summers were warm enough to melt the top centimeters of the planet's ever-present ice. In the winter, the air outside was too cold to breathe.

Arista longed for summer. She had only seen the glory of summer three times in her life. In summer, there were hikes, outdoor astronomy lessons, and geology. It was all in protective suits, but they could get out of the station, that otherwise made up their whole world.

It was going to be a long time before spring.

She knew this feeling before. They all did. It was the beginning of a déjà vu. In her seven years of life, she had had her fair share of these experiences. That fading distant sensation hit her first. Then came the déjà vu itself.

• *She was standing in a hydroponics bay. Chemical smells were floating in the air.* -

Then it faded. The room in the déjà vu looked much the same as this one, minus the vegetables. Arista could hold that image tightly in her mind and review it in detail. Others didn't bother to try to hold onto them. Father said that the déjà vus were a symptom of their accelerated mental development. It was the mind playing tricks on them. Part of her wondered about that. However, he knew much more than anyone her age did. Surely he was right about this …

Their varying schedules meant that they took breakfast and lunch when convenient. Dinner, however, was unmovable. That was Father's time to be with them all. The one large table, the only one large enough to seat all of them, was positioned in the exact center of the cafeteria. This was the dinner table. Father sat at the head of the table, as always. The most favored spots were those immediately to his left and right.

Father's attention focused at the moment on Terrill, the resident artist. Father's only requirement of this meal was that it met their nutritional needs and that all were present. Dinner conversation was light, ready to end at Father's word. Tonight, there were none. Once Father rose to go to his quarters for the evening, others could leave. Lucas wandered off first. Nigel and Salaya left together next. Arista decided to go for a walk alone.

Arista found herself in one of the storerooms. Her eyes were locked on chambers along one wall. The clear plastic tanks were empty now. The maze of hoses and tubes, connected to the backside, dangled uselessly. She reached out and touched one of the tanks –

A hand grasped her from behind. She didn't like this. There was a pain at the back of the neck. She flailed again before going rigid from the pain. The hand let go and she floated in neutral buoyancy. After time, the senseless slumber came –

This wasn't a déjà vu. This was *her* memory. She pulled her fingertips away from the cold plastic. There was no other way to explain the memory.

As she rolled her neck, she could feel a solid section of harder scar tissue …Why would it go into her skull? Who did this? Father had been the only person alive before they were born. If who was known, then why?

Father was very circumspect when it came to talking about déjà vu memories. He discouraged discussion of déjà vus among them. Father's approval meant everything, so everyone went out of his or her way to avoid triggering déjà vus or talking about the ones they had. She needed to talk to someone, but whom?

Terrell was where he could usually be found. Loose papers were scattered about his feet. He was sitting on the floor, facing the picture window. Pictures of others their age were his most common subjects. Occasionally, he went into the hydroponics bay and sketched the plants there. Even rarer, were the images of the world outside. Terrell's most exotic sketches were those not from Aden. These sketches were kept very, very private. Father might not even know of them. If Arista had not walked in at the wrong moment once, she wouldn't have known either.

Terrell was busy with another sketch. A picture of Father appeared out of the chaos of seemingly random gray strokes. Arista waited until he was finished before speaking.

"You sketch him quite a bit."

Terrell shrugged. "The image simply came to my mind, and I drew it."

"He looks younger in that picture than he does now."

"That was how I saw him in my mind."

"Could it be an early childhood memory?"

"I don't know."

"A déjà vu?"

Brief hesitation before answering with, "Yes."

"Do you still have them often?"

"Not as often as I did when I was younger."

Arista sat down on the floor beside him, wanting to be eye to eye.

"Do you still have them, Arista?"

"They still come often for me."

"We will outgrow it."

"We're all almost grown. How much longer will it take?"

At eight years old, they had the physical development of individuals in their late teens or early twenties. The differences in maturity were only due to the several months spread between the firstborn and the lastborn of their generation.

"Father says wait a little longer."

"We are adults. If déjà vus were a symptom of accelerated mental development, why do we still have them?"

"They will probably fade once the accelerated growth has stopped."

"When was the last time any of us were in a tank?"

How could they forget about the tanks, meant to pump in the necessary combinations of hormones and nutrients to keep them developing properly at the accelerated pace? Except for the youngest few, the sessions had now stopped altogether. Arista wondered if the 300% acceleration in maturation was worth losing almost a fifth of their childhood. She was glad the awkward adolescence was over, but she wished she'd had more time to enjoy the childhood.

"If our period of accelerated growth is over, then the logical conclusion is that we are fully grown," Terrill agreed.

"Earth rarely used accelerated growth techniques. We aren't some special genotype that required such. We're all descended from a normal Earth population. The only answer is that we're normal, but forced to grow up much faster."

"You sound as if you enjoyed being immature."

"There was a certain innocence that we can never get back."

"Innocence? Father has always said, 'There are no innocents in the Universe, only those who do not know to look for the blows it will deal them."

"No adult responsibility. The ability to play for hours. Don't you miss those things?"

"Adults can play games. Shall we play chess?"

"Can you have a conversation without quoting him?"

"Why? Do you think there is something wrong with that?" He looked at her as if there as something wrong with her. Anything she said could, and would, be quoted, and repeated among others until Father found out. Arista chose her only option, silence. She gently moved Terrell's sketches out of her way before getting up. She'd have to find someone else to talk to.

Lucas! She thought.

He was in the middle of doing pushups before his evening run. He looked up, startled. He looked her over, surprised that she was not in a standard jumpsuit. Instead she wore the gray shorts and shirt they all typically slept in. Furthermore, she knew, Lucas alone exercised in.

"What do you want?"

"Do you mind company when you run?"

"You can come if you can keep up."

"I think I can."

"Just make sure you have a monitor on, in case you fall behind. I don't want to have to send someone to look for you."

Arista looked self-consciously at the small chip on her elastic wristband. She looked back at Lucas. He had no locator. Then again, he claimed to have memorized the layout of the tunnel system.

They had all wandered the tunnels at times as children. It had been a favorite place for hide and seek. They had all forgotten to wear monitors at some point in the childish play. Most of them had gotten lost at least once. The longest anyone had been lost was two days and two nights. Arista was not the one to have set that record, but her worst occasion came close.

"No one will have to look for me."

"Good. And try to keep up."

The next two hours were a challenge. Lucas had greater endurance, and he knew it. When Arista slowed to a walk, he jogged in place, cajoling her. When she picked up the pace again, he sped ahead before running back. He was intentionally wearing himself out as he wore her out. After ten kilometers, Lucas brought them back to the main tunnel entrance.

"I'll leave you here to recover."

"Lucas, if you don't want company, just say so."

"It's not that I don't want company." Lucas paused, uncertain. He was trying to keep his attention away from her sweat soaked shirt. "I am not used to company, down here."

"This is your private domain." She'd meant it as a sarcastic comment.

"It is."

Arista looked down into the dark maze of tunnels, branching off into the depths of the mountains and hills around them. This dark hard rock was as much a part of the planet they lived on as the thick ice that covered the ground above them. Could this, somehow, bring back memories for Lucas? She wanted to talk.

"Does this ever bring back memories for you?"

"What?"

"When you're running, do you ever have … déjà vu?"

"Why do you ask?"

She wanted answers. Even mere confirmation that others had the same questions would be enough at this moment. Yet there was nowhere else to go, and no one else to talk to, if she pushed things too far. "No reason."

Lucas allowed her to accompany him a few more times. He even slowed his pace to accommodate her. Others noticed their new association. Rumors similar to those circling Nigel and Salaya's intimacy began. Father finally learned of the rumors and called a special meeting.

"I know that all of you have reached a state of physical maturity." There was a breathless pause in the crowd. Arista could feel the tension, *"He is finally going to tell us!"*

"However, none of you have reached a state of true emotional and psychological maturity. If you had been born on Earth, it would have taken you 20 years to reach physical maturity. It would have taken more years before you were ready to begin selecting mates."

There was a dramatic pause. "No. You will not have to wait another 20 years before you are ready for more … adult activities. However, you are not ready now. Those who think you are ready, come speak to me in private. It will be considered on a case-by-case basis. Those who cannot find the courage to speak with me should not even think about these issues." He added ominously, "You cannot even imagine the consequences of these actions."

After days of deliberations, Father allowed everyone access to the sexual education material and anatomy lessons. The gender gap suddenly became important. Some asked how they would deal with it. For Arista, another question arose. If each person were meant to pair up male to female, then three men would be left without. Their lives were so planned, how could this obvious flaw in the plan exist?

"Father, why are there more males than females?" Arista asked.

Father was surprised at her question. He thought she was going to discuss Lucas with him. "I had not planned on having so many more male genotypes."

"You could have created more females to compensate once you knew."

"I did not know the gender ratio would occur until after the births."

"Once you knew, you could have created more females from the successful genotypes that had survived birth to correct the imbalance."

"No."

"Why not?"

"There shall be only one of each of you."

He could have said that he could only handle so many of them, so he was simply postponing creation of more females. He could have said more males were needed due to their innate skill sets. His actual answer was vague. She could barely comprehend it, much less the vehemence with which he said it. Arista took her leave.

Identical twins had occurred in the human population. Humans had learned how to deal with duplicates throughout history. Cloning brought twins occurring years apart. But people had managed to deal with it. Why no clones? It had been done on Earth.

Arista ran a search of the topic. The computer traces kept her looking, though there were no official answers. It took hours since much of the file history had also been deleted. The files in question themselves had been deleted 10 Earth years ago.

The backup file she had found showed that tens of thousands of files that had been deleted at the same time. More puzzling, the records of the mass deletion had also been deleted. Considering that her generation was born after the deletion, there was only one possible culprit.

Her first question was "Why do it?" Her second was "Why hide it?" Her third question was whether or not she should bring it up to Father. She decided to ask for another opinion.

Arista and Lucas resumed their jogs. She dressed more conservatively, now mindful of the sexual tension. Arista used the jogs as an excuse for exploring the tunnels. She had developed a notion that there was something out here, waiting to be found. It had not arisen from a déjà vu moment. It was the lack of evidence now as glaring as the white tunnel lights.

Arista suggested a turn off into one of the tunnels that hadn't been used for years.

"Why go that way?"

"I'm curious about what's down there."

"That doesn't answer my question."

"How long has it been since anyone's done an inventory of what equipment is still located in these tunnels?"

"The inventory shouldn't have changed in that time."

She came up with a tag for his curiosity. "I think I've found gaps in the inventory." She had his attention. "Whether the equipment was misplaced or crushed in a landslide, I don't know. But we should find out. Who knows what's lost?"

"Why look *now*?"

"It would take these jogs and turn them into a productive use of our time."

He agreed with her reasoning. She knew better than to go into old tunnels alone and without others knowing of her whereabouts. Now there was help, and an excuse to be here.

A month later she found something. Arista persuaded him to remain silent until they had determined what they really had. They had to return several times before they had enough lights to see, and time to actually review the findings.

On one hand, she was utterly drawn to them. It wasn't simply curiosity. It was attraction mixed with morbidity. On the other hand, the information terrified her. She wanted to burn them, destroy them. Here were answers to those questions. And it horrified her.

The station here had once housed over a hundred terraformers. Arista could not understand the mindset of these people. Terraforming required decades or centuries. They left all they knew behind for a task whose end result they would not live to see. Nor would their descendants, for they would have no descendants.

Earth was concerned about the effects of radiation caused by space travel, as well as the risks of a colony forming on a world that was not capable of supporting a permanent population. Thus all the terraformers were irrevocably sterilized before leaving. Father had lied; this was not, and had never been a colony.

Most had no social attachments to Earth. How else could they come here, leaving behind all they knew for a harsh job? This world had no comforts to speak of. Money had no meaning here, so it could not be for pay. The benefits for the 50 men and 50 women who came were purely intangible. Arista thought the proper gender ratio in the first generation was ironic – it *had* been planned right the first time.

For some, it was the desire to explore. For most, it was a truly altruistic task – they could leave no better memorial behind than a living world. The records of the accident on the other hand were sketchy. The few survivors had suffered oxygen deprivation and exposure to extreme cold. The notes were increasingly incoherent until they stopped.

Terraformers used paper notebooks for diaries. It was far more private than electronic documents, that any one of a dozen others could have hacked into and read. Also, paper records could be recycled at the owner's leisure.

Father had done exactly that after the accident. He had missed only a few bits of evidence. This small tunnel had been a private refuge for engineers who had survived the dome rupture, though they eventually died of chronic health problems. They took their time here, at the end of work shifts on the geothermal power stations, to record thoughts as their minds and bodies slowly failed after the accident.

Every child wonders where it comes from. They had found out that the story they had been told was a lie. Father had cloned them from the dead terraformers. Arista looked up their files from the deleted ones she'd recovered. The names were disconcertingly familiar.

The older version of herself looked strange to her. *Ariel Stanley Derringer.* Terrill was contraction of Terrence Donovan Argyll. He had been a chemist. A note in his profile caught her attention. "*Tested high for creativity. No formal training in this area was pursued.*" Father had to have had these files. He knew Terrill could be a great artist. And he knew that the first man had not perfected the talent. So he encouraged Terrill for the first one's lack.

It all explained how Father knew their natural abilities before they themselves realized it. He already knew their potential based on these files, from the personality tests and such done by Earth on their predecessors. Predecessors? Parents? They only had one Father. Siblings? Twins? There was no appropriate word for the relationship between generations.

She found the message sent to Earth. "Dome breached. Eleven survivors, all with injuries and suffering effects of exposure to Aden's natural atmosphere." It took 20 years for

Earth to receive the message. Arista did a brief timeline in her mind. Allow for 1 year for the survivors to die, a year or two of research for Father to begin his work, five years for attempts, eight more years to the present … Earth would not receive the message for the Delta Pavonis system another four Earth years.

If Earth sent more recent messages, they weren't in this database. Arista reached out to turn off the computer screen -

Her hand hovered above the switch. A signal indicated that new data had come in from a monitoring station. A screen nearby was flooded with readings -

The others did not have déjà vus in this detail. Not that they admitted to at least. Why her? Had she been an experiment? No. That was paranoia. Reading those journals was affecting her.

They were clones. But she knew the cloning process. She'd performed it herself with plants. Except for the need to gestate children to term …but they had been brought to term in the tanks. None of this explained the déjà vus. She knew that the cloning process did not impart memories. So how did the déjà vus evolve? Would studying his original experiments explain them? That would mean studying the bodies.

Dream images of people screaming and dying, as cold useless air poured in, jolted her awake. Arista waited for the terror to subside. In the calm, she realized these images were of her dreaming mind's own making, not a déjà vu.

Perhaps it had been best that they had not known about the accident. Children had their terrors. Why let them know about a real threat? The dozen survivors had repaired the dome well enough. Father had drones to continue with the maintenance. The accident would likely not happen again. In a few years, the terraforming process would render the air outside breathable. There was still a chance the disaster could be repeated … killing everyone she knew. *It was a horrible way for me to die.*

Me? I am not Ariel! I am alive. She's dead. But ...

Arista made her way to the back corridors. It was late at night. Except for Nigel, in the clinic on the night shift, and Sheridan at the maintenance monitors, everyone else should be asleep. She had decided not to include Lucas into this investigation.

She had learned of the labs in these back corridors. Father had sealed off sections. No one had ever come to question him about it. After all, they were such logical explanations. If not for the journals, she wouldn't have known.

For the first time in her life, she was glad there were so few in her generation. It lowered the likelihood that she would encounter someone as she snuck about the halls. She did not want to answer someone else's questions right now.

Arista felt as if she were on the edge of a déjà vu. She'd never been past the door she'd jimmied open. Yet they seemed familiar. She closed her eyes and waited. She wanted to get the déjà vu over with, so she could continue in her search without distraction. After several minutes, Arista gave up.

She found the old primary research lab. It was the largest, and thus best place to search. She reached out for the door's keypad. She entered the usual door code. It didn't work. Arista was surprised. All the doors used the same one. Well, all the doors in their section of the dome. This door was probably not meant for easy access for Father's children.

An unknown four number password would have 9999 possibilities. Did she really want to stand here and start with 0000 and work up from there? That annoying feeling of an incipient déjà vu remained.

Her hand rose up of its own accord. Arista felt odd, aware of what was happening, but not fully in control. The first sequence of 0946 didn't work. The second code of 6666 opened the door. The blast of cold air from the open room brought her back from the dreamlike state.

Arista stepped inside. The lighting was dim. Arista took a cautious breath. Despite the cold, the atmosphere was the same as the rest of the station. Arista felt goose bumps. It was below freezing in here.

Equipment was scattered haphazardly. A few trays of instruments were off to the side. Arista could see cryogenic equipment along the walls. Of course, a terraforming facility had tons of plants in storage. A promising species, which could not be immediately introduced outside, could be frozen for those intervening years.

A few flashing lights in the back caught Arista's attention. She walked toward them. The green and yellow flashing sequences indicated that whatever equipment was back here was still functioning. Arista tripped on a low-lying conduit. She threw her arms forward. Her right arm caught on something and Arista fell in that direction to avoid falling on her face.

She fell across a cryogenic tank instead. The three meter long tank was the largest model they had. There were a few modifications to the standard unit. An extra set of monitors. Several added sensors whose wires snaked out from drilled holes. There most obvious modification was a small plastic window. It was covered with frost. Arista absently wiped the frost away with her hand. Then she froze. It was Nigel. No, it couldn't be Nigel. Nigel was in the infirmary right now. This was … the man Nigel was cloned from.

Arista could see two dozen other units. As she moved from unit to unit, she saw older versions of familiar faces. Why were they still here? If Father had simply wanted them cloned, he had already accomplished that. Why keep the bodies around when they were no longer needed?

At one of the last tanks, she found what she already expected to find. It was an older version of her own face. It was Ariel. Staring at that face, she felt the déjà vu sensation come back. That was impossible. She couldn't possibly remember this.

It wasn't just one déjà vu, one old memory. It was dozens. Then hundreds. They came all in one huge rush. Arista was briefly aware of sinking down to the floor, fists pressed to her forehead, trying to make the deluge stop. She couldn't understand it and she couldn't stop it. She passed out.

The maelstrom of memories was easing. It still swirled around her in her mind's eye, but it left her in a kind of calm at the eye of the storm. Slowly, details began to mesh with more recent memories. Lucas had a reason to be so driven to athleticism in this life. In his first life, an infection had robbed him of his mobility. Arista remembered the motorized wheel chair that had carried him about the terraforming complex. He had mourned that loss, and carried it with him into the next life.

The storm was slowing down. Ready to go back to her quarters, Ariel opened her eyes and found Father and Nigel leaning over her. Their faces triggered another déjà vu, a fresh whirlwind. With it, she slid back into the abyss.

The door to the lab was ripped open. Freezing air ripped through the lab. She fell back, instinctively curling up against the cold, as everything else faded away -

A harsh jolt hit her, bringing her back. Devon was leaning over her, his face covered by an environmental suit. She couldn't breathe. Darkness came again -

Father had been Devon Ashanti. They'd been sent on the same flight to Delta Pavonis, three years after the construction crew's last message reached Earth that they had completed construction of the base. When they arrived, the construction crew would be old or dead. They turned out to be dead.

The construction crew's sacrifice was something they were to repeat. Now the scientists could give their lives up for the sake of making a world live. So what if she gave up the hope of a family, that dream Devon complained about having to give up in exchange for the chance to be out here? Her life's work was guaranteed to be in the history books.

Other memories came up in a disjointed rush.

- *Faces of her parents, killed in a riot –*
- *Looking down on Earth from orbit, floating in zero gravity for the first time –*
- *Devon, smiling at her, as she continued talking about the latest promising bacterial splicing results that she had made in the lab –*

Slowly, the tide eased. With time, the rush became slow waves, with brief periods in between for the memories to be assimilated. Gradually, the sea calmed, with new memories slowly lapping up against her internal shore.

Devon/Father was still there. She asked him, "What have you done to me?"

"The answer depends upon who I am talking to."

"My name is Ariel."

"No. It's not. Your name is Arista."

"What did you do to me?"

"You died. I cloned you and the others."

"I know that already, Devon."

He had never told the children his name. He even deleted his profile from the computer. They would know nothing of him except what he told them. "You don't have enough of her memories. This … identity construct is artificial. Arista … Ariel, I used less than 10% of the original neural tissue in each of you. In your case, 20% was used. This was because the initial grafts did not seem to take." He paused. "That might account for the situation."

"Grafts of neural tissue from the dead put into the unborn."

"Yes."

"Why?"

"I'm not getting younger. I could accelerate physical development of children. That was simple. It had been done with animals for generations. I could not wait 20 years for you to grow up. I did not have the time or energy to have 19 dependent infants running about for half a decade. Not when I could have you all as my peers in less than a decade"

Devon sighed. "Most tissue was taken from parts of the brain related to skills. The grafts would create a pre-programming for different actions. Toilet training, walking, talking. It was to allow your brains to develop as quickly as your bodies. Once I helped each child perform the action once, the dormant connections became active. Walking takes months for a child to master. For each of you, it took two weeks. Other skills arose from those grafts, innate skills that had been honed on Earth in each individual. Salaya's surgical skill are a good example."

"And the déjà vus?"

"I took a chance. I took further grafts from more advanced portions of the brain, not just the motor cortex, and grafted them during growth sessions. You were all asleep anyway, and it would make so much more possible. I meant to pre-program things like the ability to read and social skills. It was successful. You were all reading within weeks. Other skills came thru in varying degrees."

"The déjà vus?"

"I knew there was a chance some memories would be transferred with the grafts. However, this environment is so different from Earth that most would never be awakened. The few concrete memories triggered were random, and easy to dismiss as leaky neurons in a growing brain. I had expected your brains to interconnect with the grafts barely enough to allow a rapid transference of skills. The few connections to whole memory sequences were minimal and would fade with time."

"The déjà vus."

"Yes. The natural pruning process of neurons should have wiped out all the deja vus as you learned skills for yourselves. You were not intended to have ... leftover memories."

"They have survived."

"Only traces. And, without further triggering of those neurons, they will fade."

"Memories make the man."

"It takes 75% of Ariel's original memories to create a reasonable replica of Ariel's original personality. At best, 50% of her most recent memories could be enough."

"I remember dying. Twice."

"That was an accident."

"My death?"

"If I knew the death-memories were stored in the part of her mind her lab experiences were, I would not have tried to transfer those skills."

"I am not Arista."

"Really? What school did you attend?" Silence. "Who was your childhood best friend?"

"Irrelevant."

"Is it? Ariel died. I tried to save your lives. I failed in that. This was the next best thing."

"You expect gratitude?"

"If I had not been on the surface on punishment duty, I, too, would have died."

"Why punishment duty?"

"Engaging in research I shouldn't have."

"Cloning. Human cloning."

"I would not have brought the clone of myself to maturity in my lifetime. I'm not that egocentric. But if the embryos already existed, then maybe they would be brought to term when the colonization effort began. I was denied the immortality of children on Earth. Should I be utterly denied that chance, when this one faint hope existed?"

Ariel couldn't answer. Never having shared that desire, Ariel couldn't relate.

"I know what Ariel's opinions in that regard were. I don't know what Arista's opinion would be. Should we ask her?"

"She doesn't matter."

"Arista had lived eight years outside the growth tanks, five years of conscious memory. That is probably more personal memory than you actually possess." Devon sighed. "You lived over 35 years. Arista has barely started her life. Are you going to deny her that chance?"

"I don't want to die again."

"Think of her as the child you never had."

"I never wanted children."

"What if Arista does? I don't know what happened that caused you to give up on continuing the species, but now that your opportunity exists ..." Ariel didn't react. "Why should you let her live? So she can continue your work. You cared about your work. Do you think Earth would send replacements for the crew after finding out we all died in an accident? If the terraforming effort is to continue, its only guarantee is if the terraformers are born here."

"Interesting logic for violating the law."

"Don't you think people whose survival depends upon success will work harder than people who came here only to escape demons on Earth?"

"You can't do anything about this. I'm here now. I remember."

"Yes. I can. I can freeze the cells that are … we'll say malfunctioning."

"That would kill me."

"It also has a chance of killing Arista. But if I don't do this, then she's lost."

"You would lose me. Again." Ariel pieced it together as the remaining memories settled in. Those he had resurrected had been friends, those he'd wished had been friends … and the woman he had been attracted to. "You wouldn't want to lose the woman you cared about."

"Yes. I admit it. Yet I have been Father to a little girl who blossomed into a young woman. My parental instincts have become stronger than the fantasy I had for you." Devon smiled gently. "My paternal bond with Arista was reciprocated. My attraction to Ariel was likely lust and never returned. I understand now that Ariel had no room for anyone in her life. I know that as Father, I could never be Arista's partner, but I am a part of her life."

"I won't volunteer for this." Ariel strained at the restraints.

"You were always so damn determined."

"So you'd kill me."

"I'm going to try to save Arista. I created her. I owe her that. I'm her Father." Devon reached out for the hypospray. Ariel began screaming. Devon quickly injected her with sedative. Long ago, he'd hoped that something like this would happen. However, he had learned in those lonely years that it was best to let ghosts fade into the darkness. For the first time in years, he cried. He had mourned the dead in those lonely years. He mourned that he had finally succeeded in bringing someone back in more than mere flesh. He mourned that his finally achieved success might cause him to fail. Leaving him to fail Ariel yet again.

He kept Arista drugged, comatose, to ensure silence as he cremated the dead. He had an obligation to the other children to protect them from the past. That was above his duty to repair Arista. Then Lucas volunteered the documents on his own accord. All evidence was destroyed.

With the cleanup complete, it was time to focus on the patient. Nigel asked, "Are you certain this will eliminate the seizures?" It was the only excuse he could give for Arista's sedation.

The overactive memory clumps were visible by MRI. If necessary, he'd destroy all recent memories. He didn't know what the end result would be. All he could do was act immediately, then wait and see. Thin needles with liquid nitrogen would destroy them.

Nor could he pray for the best. He was an atheist. Besides, if a God existed, then so might Hell. He thought the latter already existed here and now before him. He shuttered at the thought of a supernatural place of even greater anguish.

"Do you think anyone else will require this procedure?" Nigel asked.

He hated having to ask for help, but he could not do this procedure alone. "Unlikely. Arista was the last of an uncertain batch prone to these problems. The rest died in utero."

"Will the procedure have to be repeated?"

"We won't know until she awakens." Devon refused to say, "*If*". Devon had to force himself to tend to the others. None of them had had to deal with impending disability or death before. The concept was unnerving to them. He tried to focus on their emotional well-being. If Arista died, he would depend on the survivors even more for his sanity.

Lucas persuaded Salaya to let him visit. He waited until Salaya was out of earshot before saying what he needed to say.

"I don't know what we have between us. I don't understand what was driving you. Father says you were developing epilepsy. Whatever is wrong with you, I don't care what caused it, as long as you get better." He put his head down, forcing himself to remain calm. "I don't want you to die. Wake up!"

The eyelids squinted further closed before flying open. Arista tried to sit upright and was thrown back by the restraints. Arista could not talk coherently for hours. Father began several different medications. Lucas was pushed off to the side as Arista faded in and out of consciousness. Father never asked why he was there, only ordered him to stay out of the way.

Arista finally asked her first coherent question. "Where am I?"

"In the medical section."

"How long have I been here?"

"Several days."

"What happened?"

Devon watched a slow panorama of emotions cross her face. "Don't you remember?"

"No."

Devon tried to strip the emotion from his voice as he asked his next question. "What is the last thing you remember?"

The panorama of emotion sped up before slowing again. "Jogging with Lucas. No ..."

"Do you remember your name?"

"Arista." She looked startled that he even asked her the question.

Father told her what she needed to silence the questions. She'd had seizures as a result of forcing déjà vus to the surface too often. He'd done what he could to fix the problem, but she would have to do her part, too. Arista was nodding disjointedly to his words. How much did she really understand? He released the restraints but sedated her again. Nigel came in once Father gave him permission to. Lucas followed. "Is she going to be all right?" they asked nearly simultaneously.

"Only time will tell." Father looked down at his creation. He turned back to the pair. "Nigel, can you take over for me? I need to take care of other things."

"Of course."

He paused in the doorway. Lucas was sitting beside the bed. Devon watched as he picked up Arista's hand and held it. When he squeezed it gently, the semi-conscious woman returned the action. Ariel would not have done that.

Things were going to be all right.

CHURCH OF THE CALLED

Crazy cults may be more than they seem.

CHURCH OF THE CALLED

"Who are you and why are you here?"

Burke sat in a chair in front of a large antique wooden desk, an item far more expensive that he'd thought the quiet enigma before him could own. On the other side of the desk sat Jensen Ishadow, the man he knew as the founder of this group. To the side of them both was Eric O'Shay. O'Shay was legally the founder of the Church of the Called; he was the one who had put his signature to the paperwork. As a hard-hitting lawyer, that made legal sense. At least one thing in their organization made sense. Ishadow's wife was nearby, but off to the side. Whether as moral support for her husband, or for other reasons, he didn't care. Burke was here for the truth.

"My name is Samuel Burke, as you probably already know." He'd flagged his file to notify him if anyone did a background check, and there'd been one the day he'd arrived in this rural backwater area. For a people who eschewed technology, clearly they had followers somewhere he didn't know about with access to tech. Somehow someone had leaked his information or his assignment to them. Burke decided that he'd have to be straightforward to get any serious answers.

"I came to ask questions." No one else in the room seemed surprised by his statement. "Your people haven't been amenable to that in the past. Will you answer them now?"

"Ask." Ishadow seemed calm and amazingly unconcerned. Ishadow didn't talk to reporters. He never even appeared in public. Yet he smoothly offered to answer an investigator's questions? What was up their sleeves? What did they know? Or, perhaps, what had they already covered everything up?

"The incident with the gunman."

Ishadow subtly unrelaxed without moving a centimeter. The voice, however, was as smooth as before. "How did you find out about that?"

"It was too strange a story to have been made up." Burke suppressed a smile. He'd had the police report, though a reporter would have had to hunt through the rumor mill for years for any leads to the classified incident.

"He talked about it and was believed?"

"We tried to keep it quiet."

Ishadow and O'Shay had spoken at once. Burke knew he had thrown them both off guard. He smiled openly now.

"What happened?"

Ishadow nodded to no one. "Tell us what you know."

Burke began. "An assailant broke into your home with a gun. He found your wife first. She cooperated with him and promised him money that was kept elsewhere in the house. They walked through the hall, him behind her, gun aimed at her, until you stepped out of your office. He threatened to shoot if he wasn't given money. Your wife ducked out of the way as you lunged for the assailant. You lifted him off the floor, hands on his throat. You then released him. The assailant fell to the floor raving. When the police came, you told them what I'm telling you now. The man confessed. The story is that the oxygen deprivation from the neck grasp affected his brain, making him helpless, but coherent enough to cooperate with police." Burke fell silent.

"That is how it happened." O'Shay responded.

Burke let criticism color his voice. "Did you read the doctors' reports?"

Ishadow shook his head. Nothing said, and gestures could not go into a legal report.

"The man had a history of drug abuse. His criminal record was a mile long. He is now a model prisoner. Except for one thing. He is delusional. He claims an angel spoke to him and forced him to feel what his victims feel. The psychiatric ward doctor who recently examined him found no sign of concussion or oxygen deprivation. There was no physical reason for the change in personality."

Burke wanted angry justifications. Or, perhaps, violent denials. He wanted someone to say something to contradict the official testimony of a madman. He had answers, but still no real answer. Was this their plan? Something so absurd no one would believe it?

Burke went on. "He claims it grew in intensity until it reached the point where he embraced darkness over having it continue. He has nightmares about the experience. While the emotions were roaring through his mind, he also had unexplained visions.

The man happens to be an excellent artist. He has been able to draw the images that torment him."

Ishadow was now ready walk out of the room. Or throttle Burke. A thin line of control kept him there. If this group had a secret bioweapon the leader had used in his self defense, Ishadow might be upset enough to leak the answer. Burke tried to act like a reporter.

"I would like for you to try to identify some of them, if you can. I have a dozen of his drawings in my brief case." Burke handed the pictures to Ishadow. Ishadow studied each in detail, taking his sweet time, using the delay to regain his annoyingly smooth composure.

There was one in particular Burke had noted. It was a picture of a woman of mixed ancestry the assailant could not identify. The felon had seen this image many times in his visions. Burke had nicked the corner of that picture so he could identify it readily. Ishadow was hit by emotion when he reached it.

Burke asked gently, "Who is it?"

"My first wife."

"She's been dead for four years."

"Almost five," Ishadow corrected.

Burke asked his key question. "How would a man breaking into your home for the first know what your dead first wife looked like? And how would he associate the image of your dead wife with your living one?"

Tension lay heavy in the air. He watched their expressions shift in silence as if to a conversation Burke alone could not hear. The woman finally said, "Very well. Mr. Burke. This is going to take time to explain."

"And what exactly is that?"

"You have to turn off your recorder."

"What makes you think I have one?"

O'Shay flatly retorted, "You're a reporter, aren't you?" A hint of accusation lay beneath the question; they knew he was more than a reporter, but O'Shay wouldn't say that on recording.

"Is the cult a sham as well?" He saw both men nod and felt like screaming, his video card had been ruined by their security barrier. Burke felt he was on the verge of a major breakthrough "It's off."

It was the wife who answered. "The diet restrictions, prohibition on alcohol and drugs, emphasis on family - most of us practiced those things or held those values before we came here. But those of us who had a religion before still do. It is possible to be this and have your original faith." The woman glanced at O'Shay who merely shrugged at her words. She continued. "We have Buddhists, Christians, atheists, and Hindus. Most have moved on to our official semi-Buddhist faith, but not all."

O'Shay chimed in. "It was easier to get a permit for the

private school if we were a unique and separate faith."

"It's an excuse." Burke suppressed a smile. He had thoroughly studied the backgrounds of all the members of the cult. Most had lost relatives to violence or suicide, but none had criminal records themselves. They came from all races and economic backgrounds. Yet they'd joined this group. It didn't meet any extremist profile they had on record. If the bioweapon possibility hadn't come up, a man's brain scrambled with no other explanation for it, then there would have been no investigation at all.

Ishadow smiled wanly. "We are telepathic."

Burke began laughing until tears ran down his face. The irony hit him so hard he couldn't control his breakdown. He'd turned off his recording device! Then he gets the worst lie he'd heard in ages! If he'd at least got the words on tape he'd have proof these nuts were as crazy as the victim in the asylum! Maybe developing their stuff had had unplanned consequences. If only he'd had their crazy excuse on a legal recorder! It was worth the craziest excuse award the prosecutors gave, if nothing else. And he couldn't prove it!

Ishadow finally said, "Laura, please."

Burke convulsed involuntarily against the unknown; his laughter cut off abruptly as though a switch had been flipped. "What the hell just happened?"

"You needed proof." Burke ran his hands into his neck from the convulsion. How had they done that? Ishadow began again.

"Talent has its price. As children, the ability is subconscious."

"Then why all the bad luck?"

"As adolescents, when we learn how to control it, we can make mistakes. You can tell if someone intends to do harm, but not if it is directed towards you. When you react in self-defense, you reach out and touch their mind. Some react by turning the aggression off. But half the time it is released then and there at you. That's how my wife died. The effort to redirect the aggression caused it to be directed doubly at her."

O'Shay jumped in. "If someone else is depressed, the emotion gestalts. Suicide seems the only option. Sometimes others come to realize subconsciously they are being manipulated and come to dislike you, even if they do not know why. In time, it grows to violence. It is why we are prone to being murdered if we don't commit suicide first." It was almost too much to believe despite the demonstration. Almost.

Laura frowned. "Burke, I'll try to help you understand. Imagine sitting in a room. You cannot see anything. People's thoughts are voices coming through the walls, ceiling, and floor. With distance, the volume of each fades. The more intense the emotion, the louder the voice is. If someone near you is emotional, you hear it all. They are so loud you cannot think your own thoughts."

"You cannot talk to them. They cannot hear you. If you are familiar with the voice, it will come through clearly because you are familiar with it. You can focus on voices the same way you can listen to one person in a crowed room. Focus on a voice, and the rest fade into background noise. If there is physical contact, it is even stronger. A casual touch will break down concentration ... any barrier you built up." Thoughts of what might happen during physical encounters welled up in his mind. Laura added, "We do not have intimate relationships with those not like us."

Ishadow picked up where his wife left off. "You learn things you do not want to know. They lose all secrets and never know it. Why try to get to know them? You already do." Ishadow's tone lightened as he smiled at his wife. "With another psychic, you can control the depth of contact. In marriage, it allows for more intimacy, communication, and emotional stability than the non-talented can ever have."

O'Shay concluded. "If we raise our children in a community, they are safe. If they choose to face the world, at least they had the chance to reach their potential and not risk their lives doing it. Furthermore, there is a safety in numbers."

"How many of you are there?" Burke's voice was low.

"We started with 20. There are now 58 adults and 23 children." O'Shay shrugged. "Only one in a million or so has the ability, so there are few to recruit. We choose quality over quantity, so there is no breeding like rabbits."

Burke was having difficulty absorbing it all. His mind was reeling. "You said you could manipulate...."

"Only a few can do so effectively," Laura answered.

"Have you manipulated me?"

"Only when you were laughing, but I have been listening." Burke remembered his laughter being cut off.

"O'Shay, you had the highest confession rate of any lawyer, ever."

O'Shay affected the tone of a lecturer. "If a thief feels any guilt or reservations, it is easy to - influence - someone into confession. It helps put them behind bars. I consider it my fair share of community service."

"What happened to the gunman?" Burke asked quietly.

Ishadow spoke. "It was self-defense. The images he saw were feedback from me. He was willing to kill Laura, and I was not willing to lose her. I could not kill him without risking an investigation we could not afford. So I did the only other thing equally effective. He will never harm anyone else, ever."

"What are you going to do with me?" One was listening to his very thoughts. The other two could make him do anything they wanted. Burke felt paranoia rising in his mind.

"Samuel Burke!" Burke jolted forward in his chair at the

woman's voice. She had used the exact same tone teachers used to make him behave. "Sit down." The tone was less severe. Burke closed his eyes against despair.

"Jensen, what are we going to do with him?"

Burke felt her words both easing and heightening his fears. "I'm leaving." Burke rose to his feet.

"Sit down now!" Laura and O'Shay said, simultaneously. Burke's body obeyed against his will. O'Shay took the briefcase. Within thirty seconds, Laura had the tape in her hands. Burke watched another mental conversation between the three. His legs would still not obey him. How could he put this in his report? How could he explain being held against his will without the use of physical restraints? And no recording … Burke closed his eyes again.

Laura spoke in a cordial tone. "Burke, I suggest you relax and get comfortable. Take off your jacket and tie."

"No." Burke forced finality into the word. At least his voice was his own.

The woman inhaled slowly. "Let me try first. If I cannot get through that way, I'm leaving the room. I don't want to watch." Burke flinched when he felt his body move against his will. He felt himself rise, take off his jacket and tie, and sit back down. A damned puppet on strings. "What name would you prefer I use, Burke?"

"Do I have a choice?" Let sarcasm show, he told himself.

"Yes, you do." She was silent for a moment. "Fine. Burke, picture the white room I described earlier." Then, angrily, "O'Shay, stay out of this." The tone fell, pleasant again "It would be easier if you tried to cooperate."

"Why? I don't want my brains to be scrambled."

Burke's dismay broke through when she laughed heartily. "Very good! I didn't know you had seen that campaign against drugs commercial. 'This is your brain, this is drugs, and this is your brain on drugs.' Pssst, egg is put into the frying pan and sizzles." Burke tried to shake off the returning despair. She was reading his mind.

"Back to the matter athand." O'Shay's voice.

"The white room. You visualized it before, do so now. Breathe in, out, in."

"I can't."

"Burke!" It was a parent's tone of reprimanding a child. Suddenly, the image materialized in his mind. She dropped back to a conversational tone. "You are sitting on the floor, comfortably, with your eyes closed. You know where you are, right in the middle." The tone lowered, carrying a note of admiration. "Now open your eyes there."

Burke opened his imaginary eyes, though it was almost voluntary. He was sitting cross-legged on the floor, staring at his imaginary hands. He could no longer feel his body. "Look at me," Laura said.

He looked up to see Laura sitting in front of him in a Zen lotus position "Very few non-talented can get this far. You have a bit of talent. Is that why you volunteered for this assignment? Or to get recognized?"

"Stop heckling me."

"I'm not."

"Do not fry my brain!" As if he had any choice in the matter.

"Burke, listen to me. There have to be some mental blocks in your mind before we can let you go. Even if you promise not to talk about what you have learned and already knew before you came, you could spill it next time you got drunk. You could be interrogated. You could undergo polygraph and have it leak out. If you want to go home, you have to cooperate with me."

Burke kept his voice steady. "What if I do not cooperate?"

"The memory barriers would be put in place whether you cooperate or not. There would have to be rerouting to keep you from noticing the barriers regardless. It could all come apart if you fought against it after the barriers were in place. We put in safeguards so that if the barriers come down, it would drive you insane. You'd go insane anyway if the mental barriers eroded and the synaptic leakage interfered with your conscious mind. If you fight, putting the barriers in would be harder for us and for you, but all the negative consequences are yours."

"Would it be painful?"

"You cannot have fear or rage or denial about this. If it is a choice between a risk to your sanity and a threat to my family, you lose."

"So?"

"At least here, I have a chance to see old age with my husband, to see my kids grow up."

"I don't care." Burke's chest was heaving for air that refused to come. Her rage was a physical pressure on his chest. He heard her say, "No need to come to my defense. I'm fine." His breath returned. He felt her ease him back to a sitting position.

"Can you breathe now?"

Burke nodded jerkily. He craved escape more than sanity. "What does it take to put these ' barriers ' in place?"

"If you cooperate, you can watch - or hear - what we do and give your own suggestions. It is a cross between a command, a suggestion, and writer's block." She shrugged.

"Get it over with."

"Are you certain?"

"Yes." Burke mentally braced himself against whatever was coming.

"Thank you for cooperating." The irony of it was a hard slap to his ego. "I will be careful and will have help from others. No more will be done than absolutely necessary." A hand pushed him back into the chair. "There is no need to hold your breath."

Burke could not immediately describe what he felt. The pain was minimal, but nightmarish visions began to form. He was aware of what was being done, but was not involved in it. A baritone voice stated clearly, "You will not talk about any of what you have learned today or knew beforehand. You will not write or express it in any form to anyone unless it is to someone you know to be one of us." The litany went on, hammered down through consciousness and even deeper than that. Finally, it stopped. "It was easier since you did not fight."

Burke's vision was blurred, body shaking and damp with sweat. Burke doubted he could have stood. Someone put a glass to his lips. Burke drank greedily.

"Better?" someone asked.

Burke nodded jerkily. "Are you done?"

"Not yet."

"Get it over with", Burke said as he braced himself. He fought tears that didn't come.

Pressure built up slowly in his mind. There was no assistance when he instinctively struggled against the sensations this time. Burke wondered if Laura had indeed left the room, if this was the part she refused to witness. Burke felt hands clamp down on his upper arms. "I can't," Burke murmured.

"If you do not get up, I will force you."

Burke forced himself up. Eyes glazed over, he ignored the other three. Once past the door, he made decent speed away from the building and toward the desert Away from where his comrades were waiting.

Ishadow calmly watched the man go. His colleagues

would find him, eventually.

Laura finally asked, "Why tell him so much if you weren't going to put him in a coma?"

"He was too healthy to be comatose without too many questions. Besides, hun, everyone has to have a confession once in a while."

"That's silly," O'Shay spat.

"Hey, we're a religion, right?"

BREATHING ROOM

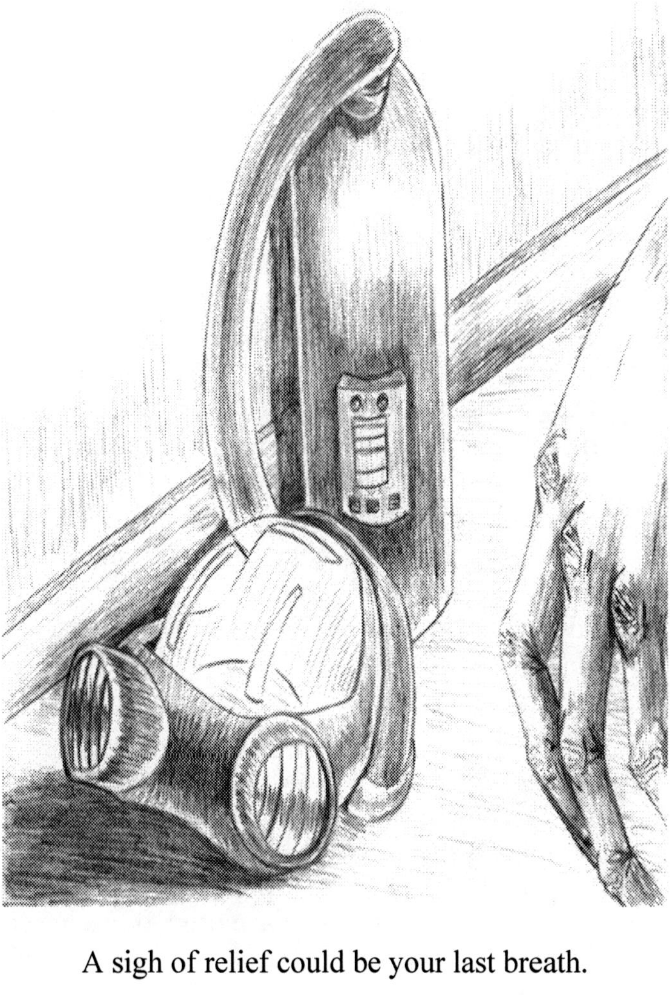

A sigh of relief could be your last breath.

BREATHING ROOM

Rochelle fell in time to see the wall of poisonous vapors. It billowed forward, reaching ugly deadly tentacles for her. The acrid smell burned her throat, Rochelle sat upright, clutching her chest, gasping for breath. The oxygen monitor by her bed glowed a comforting green. It was just a nightmare.

It was the same nightmare every night. She went outside to escape the nightmare. The beauty of the foothills of the Rocky Mountains comforted her. Safety in serenity was what they'd hoped for. But Jeremy had left her in the cabin. Jeremy was cautious this one time and didn't take off without his family. That decision saved them from his fate.

The Pacific Rim Project was intended to control earthquakes. Scientists would trigger little quakes along all the major faults to prevent the big quakes. Several minor faults in the Pacific Rim were released at once on one day. Mother Nature didn't agree. Within hours, ten volcanoes had erupted, causing tsunamis and subsequent quakes far larger than any the world had ever seen. The movement along the plates unsettled every volcano that would have blown in the next century. The unexpected aftershocks damaged the control equipment. There was no longer a way to control the quakes, and no way to stop the eruptions. Every active volcano on the planet belched at least once, and the deadly fumes enveloped everything below four thousand feet before a day had passed. Lava started fires, which only added to the problem. Mudslides cut off routes people at lower elevations could have used to reach safety.

Tibet was still habitable, though overwhelmed by refugees from India and China. The Rocky Mountains were high enough; mostly rural zones surrounded by parks prevented the starvation of Southeast Asia. Ski lodges in the Alps radioed in from time to time, echoing the same hungry story. Famine took more of the survivors. Many Andean cities emptied into the countryside, only to have the indigenous folk resort to human sacrifice to appease the gods and their followers' appetites. Lack of fuel and power took many the next few winters. No one knew how many were still alive, but it was a tiny fraction of the original 8.5 billion.

The major fear now was that an updraft from lower elevations would carry up clouds of deadly fumes from below. You couldn't see or hear it coming. You couldn't smell it until it was too late. Oxygen monitors were a cruel joke; they just told someone that the fume levels were high enough to destroy their lungs. By the time a person got a gas mask on, the damage was done. Another exposure or two would be fatal.

Jeremy had wanted children. Rochelle also wanted them, eventually. She was reluctant to do so in this uncertain world. That so many of the survivors were rugged outdoorsmen, who leered lustfully at her, only shut her down further. She would have volunteered as a teacher or sitter if the chance arose. But it didn't. Children had more lung surface area in proportion to their body size than adults. Thus, they were more vulnerable than adults. She hadn't seen a child since the last winter and the last rounds of lung infections.

Rochelle knew the Earth looked like Venus now. Her hand hovered over the gas mask by the door. She decided to go without it. She spotted the space station. The space station had been so damn close to self-sufficiency … if they had reached self-sufficiency, they could wait out this disaster. A couple hundred people who could do nothing but watch. Amateur radio operators cranked up generators and beamed signals up, but there had yet to be a signal back. All they had to do to preserve the species was to be able to wait it out. Like those left on Earth.

But for how long? They couldn't migrate much higher. Food, at least here, was not as bad as it could have been. Hunters were the only reason people ate every day. Yet the scarcity of humanity ensured its longer-term survival. If more people had survived in the area, then the wild life would have declined to extinction under the increased hunting pressure as it had further south.

Rochelle had tried working with snares. She knew she didn't have to. Men gave meat to her when she came into town. She knew why, too. It was the same reason why there were no children. Women had more lung surface area than men. Children died first, then sick and elderly adults, and then healthy women. Men survived the longest. Most people living out here were retirees or middle-aged couples that took up catering to the tourists as a second career.

The fact that she was unattached only added to the attention. So she stayed out at the cabin, miles from town, as long as she could stand it. It only made the locals more attentive – the cabin gave her an attractive dower. Five bedrooms, two bathrooms, a generator, an indoor water pump, and a septic system added to her alluring enticement. Jeremy had had his doubts about arranging their "vacation" until Rochelle explained her doubts about the project, and why this was a perfect place to wait it out. His family had had survivalist roots, and they had come to fruit in the building of this place. Jeremy relented, called it a "vacation" because the government didn't let anyone travel if they said they were evacuating. Jeremy took her here before returning for his sister.

As an only child, Rochelle couldn't understand Jeremy's insistence that he HAD to get his sister up here, especially since his half brother was in the area. The sister wouldn't come without her husband. That idiot brother-in-law had delayed and complained and bellyached until it was too late. Rochelle would have either left the pair behind, or dragged the sister here unwillingly.

Even if Jeremy had been unable to fly and had tried to drive up, his gas mask only had canisters to last two weeks. She knew that hospitals with infectious disease units and military facilities could protect hundreds of people from the unbreathable air. If the dying didn't break their way in and kill those who still had a chance.

After six months, she knew he wasn't coming. So she went into town to see if anyone else was left. Verishay Point had been founded after the turn of the millennium. It had 5000 people in the winter tourist season, 1200 residents in the summer. About 1000 were there when she'd gone into town the first time. It was down to 600 now. That included the few refugees from lower elevations before they all died. They suffered from chronic fatigue, malnutrition and dehydration. If you're worried about breathing, you forgo eating if it risks the seal on your mask. Some had breathed that air in threshold amounts, not enough to kill them immediately, but enough to rob them of lung function. They could be cured with a lung transplant; but there were no hospitals.

The only doctor had been one of the few men Rochelle could talk to without being propositioned every other sentence. Eventually, seeing patient after patient die was too much for him. Rochelle found him dead in his office on what should have been a social visit. It was blamed on a combination of pills. Lucas had offered her his condolences.

It was ironic that her love's brother Lucas was also town sheriff. He had the same sandy blonde hair as his younger brother. Unfortunately, he saw Rochelle as his inheritance. He let her keep the cabin only to keep it occupied.

She'd gone into town once a month to get supplies. If she missed a regular visit, Lucas came out on his methanol-fueled truck to check up on her. It saved her the trip if not the haranguing.

Methanol fuel came from the brewery outside of town. She was down to one drum of the stuff. She needed to get more while there was more to get. If she stayed, Lucas would come. If he came, he might not leave for a long time. If she went, she might avoid him altogether. Maybe. She didn't want to leave safety, despite the heavy pall of memories. But it was too far to safely walk.

She went out and got in the truck. The local bar was populated with most of the able bodied men. Beer was one thing there was no shortage of yet, with the brewery still open. Credit cards were stapled to the wall, useless decoration now. Coins made of real metal were still accepted. Rochelle nodded to the bartender as she stepped in. The man smiled at her as he looked up from the coins he was counting. "What can I get you?"

"Directions to the restroom."

The bar tender's face fell in dismay. He then forced himself to a smile. "In the back, on the right." The men's restroom was still the men's restroom. The women's restroom had been turned into a men's. There were few women left. Even fewer came into bars.

As she was washing her hands, she heard a sound. Looking down, she could see a fiber optic cable being sneaked through. She grabbed the cable and yanked it forward. There was a sharp "whump". She threw the door open. Three men scrambled back. She walked past the voyeurs without comment.

Her truck was untouched. Rochelle went down the street to the local bookstore. It was one place of female refuge in Verishay Point. Mrs. Verishay was the daughter-in-law of the environmentalist the point was named for. Mrs. Verishay never asked for Rochelle to pay for books. She had once joked that she had more business on the days Rochelle showed up than the rest of the month combined. Rochelle would often stay and talk to Mrs. Verishay for hours about the books she'd read. There had been little else to do after the disaster. Sometimes someone dropped off meat in payment. Mrs. Verishay didn't starve.

The bookstore door was ajar today. She walked up to the door and opened it. She called out. No answer. Rochelle heard footsteps behind her. She turned to find Lucas standing there. "What are you doing here?"

"I could ask you the same question."

"I drop by the bookstore when in town. What are you doing here?"

"I thought looting might have begun."

"Why on Earth would there be looting?"

"With Mrs. Verishay death, there's no reason not to, except my say so."

"What did she die of?"

"Officially? Or unofficially?"

Rochelle felt loss. Mrs. Verishay had one of the few people here she had actually connected with. There was a slight twinge of fear. Children first then women, was the order of death. "Can we talk about this in private?"

Spectators were starting to pay attention to them. Alpha male with the widow he'd been pursuing … fodder for the rumor mill, the only remaining source of entertainment. "Very well."

The jail cells were empty most days. There was little tolerance for criminals, and even fewer resources to have them locked up. Lucas had presided over many executions. On better days, he locked up troublemakers who needed to cool off, before release in the morning.

"Well, we're in private."

"Did she die of natural causes? Or was it lung failure?"

"You don't need to worry about that. She was an old woman."

"What is the real cause of death?"

"Mrs. Verishay did have lung degradation."

"Do you know what that means?"

"I can guess."

"This means it isn't really safe anymore."

"You are free to move higher up." He suggested. *As if she needed his permission.*

"Where? In case you haven't noticed, there isn't any civilization any higher up. What's next? Living in caves, off berries and squirrels?"

"I think most people realize death is coming whether we like it or not. It is simply an issue of what we do until then and how we go." Her almost brother-in-law shrugged as if life and death no longer mattered anymore.

Losing Jeremy had made her consider joining him in the afterlife. But she knew that he would have wanted at least one of them to live. As long as one of them was left, the memory of the other would still exist in the other's mind. So she held on. This cavalier statement, from a man she considered one of the more stable elements in the remnants of civilization, was shocking. What next? Mass suicides so no one went alone?

"I don't think I'll be coming into town anymore. Would it be all right for me to grab a few books from Mrs. Verishay's store before leaving?"

Lucas seemed about to say no. He then gave her permission. He escorted her to the store. Rochelle grabbed five cases of books. Those she didn't want to read could be used as fuel. "Where is she buried?"

"In the cemetery. You can't miss it. It is the only grave with fresh flowers on it." Rochelle held on to a little hope. Other women still survived, because most men wouldn't have bothered with flowers.

There were more than 20 fresh graves. Most had no markers. The fresh dirt underneath a double tombstone could identify a lucky few. At least their loved ones buried them. Most people got buried, no marker, no flowers, maybe a ceremony. Fortunately, this place had too few people to have mass graves.

Mrs. Verishay's grave was the only one decorated. A few dandelions had been recently placed. Rochelle sat down. "I wanted to let you know that I feel a loss knowing you're gone. I don't know if that is significant. I hope it is enough, because my mourning is all I have to offer you." It was time to go home. Rochelle said her final good-byes.

Rochelle spent the next two months stocking supplies. She hiked out to gather. Juniper berries, pine nuts, and wild greens. Everything she could identify as edible was gathered. She had six months worth of supplies. But winter seemed close by. She needed more supplies. Yet she wasn't willing to go to town to get free sides of venison. When she was done, Rochelle figured that she had a year's worth of supplies. She double-checked the electrical system before turning on the freezer. Jacob's thermoelectric generators worked beautifully.

Rochelle heard someone drive up one afternoon. She walked up to the peephole. It was Lucas. She opened the door. "I didn't believe you when you said you weren't coming back into town." Rochelle said nothing. "I heard there was an incident in the bar. Is that why you aren't coming back?" She remained silent. "I can make those idiots apologize, if that's what you want."

"It isn't just the incident in the bar. It's just not worth the risk."

"So you'd live all alone out here?"

"It's safe."

"Everyone knows where you live."

"It's safer."

"I can keep you safe." Rochelle shrugged at his statement. "I didn't know how much fuel you had. I wondered if you got yourself stranded …"

"I might have enough for one more trip."

"I brought another 55 gallon drum. I also brought along a few sacks of barley. They're distributing the last of the grain. I thought you'd want some."

"Thank you." Meat and fruit and fish would have been a real treat … she'd had been glad to have the variety. But beggars can't be choosers.

"Where can I leave it?"

"The middle of the living room is fine. I'll put it up later."

Lucas looked at her as if she was crazy. Later? Why not now? Then he went back and began unloading. Rochelle estimated that he brought 200 pounds of barley. Lucas then went back out and brought in a large box. "Most of Mrs. Verishay's stuff has been distributed. Most of the books are getting used as fire starters and kindling. I saved this box. I decided it was better that you had it. You're the only person who still seems to read."

"I appreciate the thought."

"I brought some wild turkey with me. If you're interested, that is."

In that moment, he was like every other man in Verishay Point. Here's meat. Trade you? You know what you can offer me … "Look, Luke, thank you for coming up here. But I don't need the meat. I don't need anything else. I appreciate you coming up here, but I don't need you watching over me. Please. Leave."

There was stunned silence. How could she turn down the alpha male? He couldn't comprehend it. Rochelle closed the door and locked it behind him. He stood out on the porch for a long time with his back to the door. Was he waiting for her to change her mind? Was he deciding whether or not to turn around, pound on the door, and demand to be let in? Finally, he left her alone.

Winter came. Luke didn't return. Rochelle reread her old books before starting on the last batch Lucas had left her. The snow piled up outside. It was a security blanket for her. Anyone who wanted to get to her had to cross the snow and dig their way down. By then, she'd have a shotgun aimed at them.

She was going through the habits of living even when life itself was being snuffed out. *As long as one of us remembers, the other isn't dead.* She spent the days flipping through Jacob's family's albums.

She gazed admiringly at the grandfather who built this place to survive World War IV. Rochelle saw the faces of those five children – including Lucas and Jeremy - growing up and the grandfather and his wife growing older. He had been so adamant that they would come up here as a family when they had kids. The same way he had been raised. Like the family Lucas wanted her to provide him with.

The well started gurgling. Yet water still flowed. Rochelle went downstairs into the basement to check the pipes. An oily residue had formed on the pipes. The Teflon seals kept it from affecting the water supply. Rochelle went back upstairs, too exhausted to care.

She didn't know how long she'd slept. She tried to sit up and fell back down. What was wrong with her? Rochelle rolled over in bed. There was a thick layer of yellowish gas on the floor. Rochelle stared at it, unbelieving. Was she dreaming? This wasn't her normal nightmare …

Slow horror crept into her awareness. She was awake, if impaired. The pipes! The sludge on the pipes in the basement! She'd been pumping up liquefied sludge along with her water. The water flowed on the inside of the pipe, filtered by those World War IV grade water filters. The gas particles escaped and solidified. With the cold humidity of a dying heater, it settled into a fog in the basement. When she'd turned on the generator the night before, the chemical fog expanded as it warmed, and came upstairs.

She could see the yellowish-brown haze. Why hadn't she smelled it? She'd acclimated to it. Rochelle could feel fluid in her chest. Death couldn't be far away. She coughed, spitting up yellowish phlegm. She coughed up more of it. She could remember nightmarish images from her dreams. Eight billion plus people had died this way. Her lungs would be closing up any minute. She'd drown in her own fluids.

She was still breathing. She was coughing out yellow gunk. Rochelle forced herself up and out of bed. Her muscles ached. She had to get to the living room. The gas mask was there. She needed that gas mask. She crawled to the living room. She pulled herself upright to get the mask. Her hands fumbled with the connections. Finally, she had it on. While trying to adjust the filters, she passed out again.

Thirst brought her back. Rochelle sat up, parched. She could also feel the oily residue inside the mask. Putting it on hadn't helped her at all because she hadn't done it right. Rochelle forced herself up to the door. She opened it, hoping the fresh air would save her.

There was a similar haze outside. Either a long lasting updraft had brought the haze to this altitude or the worldwide levels had finally reached here. Frustrated, Rochelle pulled off the gas mask. She got back out to the garage. She had to fumble to get the door to open against the yellow snow. She then got in the truck and started driving.

Verishay Point was wrapped in the yellow fog. Rochelle stopped the truck in front of the sheriff's office and got out.

Rochelle's foot hit something on the way in. It was one of the town drunks. Dead. Rochelle leaned forward and realized he'd been dead for a while. Maybe days. She started looking for Lucas.

He was locked in one of his own cells. He was surrounded by bodies crumpled on the floor. Their hands were on the bars as if they were the prisoners. There was a gas mask over his face. He'd locked himself in the cell to keep others from taking away his air supply. His skin was still white, though a yellow residue was forming on it. His chest seemed to still be moving, but the rest of him wasn't. He was alive, yet he was still dying. She searched for the emergency keys to the cell.

She got the door open and pushed the dead out of the way. Then she pulled Lucas' limp body to the truck. She started driving up an old logging road. It also led to higher elevation. She didn't check up on Lucas. All she could think was to get to higher ground. If he were dead, she'd strip the body and bury him. Her engine sputtered at the dwindling fuel.

Finally, the air cleared. It was getting colder, too. She parked in an old mill that had its doors wide open. It was a minimum of shelter, something with a roof and four walls. She pulled him inside and closed the door. The building was scant protection of bare sheet metal walls. It was, however, warmer than outside, and kept the wind from reaching them. Rochelle pushed Lucas onto an ancient couch. She then lay down beside him and fell asleep.

She woke up at hearing an unfamiliar sound. It was Lucas, trying to get his facemask off. She began helping him.

He began gasping for breath, wild eyed. He suddenly grabbed her shoulders and began shaking her. "Wake up!"

"I am awake."

She repeated it until his litany changed. "Are you real? Are you really here?" As he shook her, Rochelle felt a deeper awakening. She'd been suffering from oxygen deprivation too, not really functioning. If she'd been unimpaired, she wouldn't have gone into town looking for others. But the exposure hadn't killed her. Had the levels just not reached fatal levels for her? But if it had killed everyone else, did that mean that what was fatal for her was a higher level than was fatal for everyone else?

"Yes, I'm here."

"Where are we?"

"Higher elevation."

"The alarm sounded. I grabbed my air filtration mask and stuff. When other people started looking for masks, they realized there weren't enough masks or filtration canisters for those with masks. I had 4. I had to lock myself in a cell to keep from losing them. Oh, God!" Lucas began shaking. "I killed them. I let those people die because I wouldn't give up -!"

"What kept you alive all that time would have meant a slower death for everyone, including yourself."

"I thought of going and getting you after everyone else died. But I thought you would have already gone for higher ground. You would have moved on. But Kennedy … he killed people for their used filters. But he had a bad mask. He stood by that cell door for hours; it leaked and it was killing him. He was waiting for me to come out so he could get my good mask. He lived a day at least. By the time he died, I was too weak from thirst to get out. Thank you for coming back for me. If you hadn't, I would have died in that cell."

"I never left home for higher ground."

"What?"

She explained the water pump problem. No mask, at least not until it was otherwise too late. He stared at her with an expression of disbelief and horror. She should have died, but she hadn't. "Where's your mask now?"

"In the truck."

Lucas turned her face side to side. "You're not wheezing."

"I was disoriented in the haze."

"The levels were lethal. Everybody else from town is dead or fled."

"You're certain?"

"The sensors said it was lethal all the way up to 7000 feet."

It was her turn for hysteria. "You're joking, right? That means we might be lethally exposed, because I don't know what elevation this is."

"I don't have a sensor here, but we'd be dead if it was lethal."

"I coughed up yellow residue back at the cabin. It was thick yellow gas there like it was in town. I had a mask on, but didn't do it right because of the exposure. I was exposed. Lethally exposed. But I'm still alive. My breathing doesn't mean you're safe."

His face went white. "How?"

"I don't know."

Her old flame's words echoed: You're one in a billion. He'd meant it as a soul mate, but it had a new meaning. Sometimes survival was merely having the right genes in the right combination; winning the genetic lottery. Maybe she wasn't completely immune, but had somehow built up immunity. How didn't matter. What did matter was that she wasn't alone.

"Do we need to get to higher ground?"

"Yes." Lucas checked his gas mask before putting it back on. "My air filter is almost used up. We need to get up to at least 8000 feet."

"I don't want to live in a cave."

"We don't have to. There's somewhere we can go."

The ski lodge had been home for a hundred refugees at the start of the disaster. Violence, suicide, and disease had reduced the numbers. There were only a dozen people left. They accepted Lucas and Rochelle without question. No one had reached their location for nearly a year. The high death rate had left them with plenty of food. The two survivors were welcomed with open arms.

Lucas required weeks to recover from the exposure. Their doctor – a former nursing student - checked out Rochelle. He gave her a clean bill of health. No sign of oxygen depravation. No sign of the residue in her lungs. They said her mask had worked perfectly. Rochelle never said anything otherwise, and Lucas was too drained to talk at all.

The next years were slow. The green house effect from the gasses was a godsend. The high elevations still had thin air, but it was no longer as cold. Plants started growing on the formerly snow-capped peaks. Surviving wildlife moved up and into the arms of the hunters.

Evan and Lizella were outside playing when an updraft came. Rhiannon, her two year old, was asleep on a blanket outside. There were no masks for the children, barely enough for the adults. The alarm sounded. Lucas hobbled outside, trying to cover the children's faces with something, anything, as Rochelle sought to carry them to shelter.

Evan and Rhiannon were fine. They showed no ill effects from their exposure. Lizella, however, had collapsed before Lucas could get to her. The doctor worked feverishly before she died. The doctor stared mutely at the other two children, trying to find out why they and their mother were fine. If the alarm had been false, Lizella would not have died. If it were true, there had to be an explanation for a woman and two children surviving. Rochelle had to tell them what had happened so long ago. Two of her three had inherited her good genes.

Eventually, her next children played out the genetic lottery. Half, like Lizella, did not carry her good genes. All survivors were all somewhat resistant now. Whatever happened, the few survivors now had survivor's genes. The kids who survived would survive, and pass those unknown genes to their children.

Rochelle was staring at a globe. People still flourished in Tibet. Enough of that region had been a high enough altitude that those who did not starve were safe. Civilization existed there. Here, there were only a few remnants. But the Tibetans were not being forced by nature to adapt. They would stay up high until the mists faded. The latest data from the space station, per their new radio that Rochelle had salvaged from the lowlands, said that would be generations from now. Tibetans still died from updrafts. The world would belong to those who were fit for it.

The volcanoes had finally stopped. But the chemicals released would take centuries to break down. Fungus and a few tolerant plants made up the bulk of the world. Animals were probably gone, except for these high reaches. Fish that were chemically adapt, but Rochelle would probably never see the ocean again. She was tolerant, but that tolerant. The ocean was at sea level, part of terra incognita. Perhaps Rhiannon's grandchildren would see it.

Survival of the fittest

Does survival of the fittest always mean survival of the species?

SURVIVAL OF THE FITTEST

Conifers blended into a green blur as the miles melted away beneath the tires. Static sprayed from the radio, the noise my only companion. It was growing gray on the horizon, a warning that deep black of night was coming. As I came around a sharp bend, my headlights hit two bundled forms running across the road. I slammed on the breaks. The truck spun to a stop as the antilock breaks kept me from losing total control on the ice. The first figure continued running. The second tried to jump out of the way and was hit.

Just as I was getting out of the truck, I paused. Why would two people be running around in the pre-dawn cold? No, it would be safe. The dart gun now in my hand should allow me to handle any trouble. The bundled figure lay sprawled across the road. The man was wearing four layers of clothing. If I was going to check for injury, he was going to have to be in some sort of shelter first.

He barely fit in the back seat, but at least it was above freezing in the cramped space. His ribs were not the stark outlines - but he was not starving. That was promising in many regards. I bound his likely cracked ribs and injured shoulder before drifting into a light sleep.

I woke as my seat was thrown forward. The sudden commotion came to an as abrupt stop. His light green eyes contrasted vividly with his dark skin as he sat up to face me. Mixed race. Anglo, Native American, and maybe other ancestry. Awareness seeped into them slowly. "Thank you for bothering to stop."

"You could have died of your injuries if I hadn't."

His eyes took in every detail, his ears every sound, like a caged animal seeking escape. Yet his voice was even and controlled. "I owe you."

"I'm the one who hit you." I suppressed a frown. I didn't know this man or his feuds. "Who were you chasing?"

"A threat."

"Are you alone?"

He paused. Was he going to lie? "No. My tribe ..."

"I didn't know of any tribes in the area."

"We came south as it grew colder."

There was an uneasy silence. We all knew that story. He began to dress and hissed when he knocked his shoulder against the seat. "Are you going anywhere in particular?" He asked. I shook my head. "Are you alone?" To answer meant admitting I was alone, but so did silence.

"Are we far ..." His expression silenced me. My hand gripped the dart gun's handle. "You tell me first: What were you doing out here?"

"Hunting." His eyes flicked to my hand, my face, my hand.

"Get out."

He carefully slid around the seat. He scrambled out the door. When he glanced over his shoulder as he walked into the shadows, the green eyes glowed briefly before he vanished into the conifers.

I started the engine and headed home. The foreign green eyes haunted me home.

Nothing in my cabin was disturbed.

Canned goods were visible in the cabinet. My garden still grew below the reinforced skylights. Potatoes, onions, cress, peppers, and tomatoes reached toward the distant and failing sun. The utility room door was open, affording a view of the still. I poured some of the alcohol from it into the propane tank to cook with in the morning. More was poured into a kerosene lamp and lit. Tomorrow, I'd have to chop more wood for the fire and for wood alcohol. I was self-sufficient and able to meet all my needs, but alone since Donovan had been shot by marauders. After the cold began, people became scarce. The species was endangered.

Hunting, he'd said. Hunting what ... or, rather, whom? I couldn't help but wonder if cannibalism was becoming an ultimate last resort. My drives had been a signal to all that I was out here, and to any trackers, where I stayed. But Donovan was dead. I fought the urge to stay safe even as I counted the canned goods day by day. Alone or not, both ways were likely death.

The days no longer crawled by. Since the encounter, I had more energy. Before that, only my drives got me motivated enough to get out of bed. Depression led to sleep that saved energy, but it was a start towards the grave.

Someone was knocking on the door. I grabbed the dart gun. I unlocked the door despite the danger. Loneliness was making me crazy enough to risk my life. Accepting the invitation, the door opened. The stranger entered. I shut the door behind him. He put a pistol and knife on the counter and held his hands in plain view.

"Why are you here?"

"His tracks led here." He smiled grimly. "You certainly drove a long route back."

"Why are you after this person?"

Green eyes glowing faintly, he frowned. "He has been trying to pick us off one by one. It's self-defense."

"I don't care. Just keep me out of it." He grinned at me. "You act like a wild animal." Poof, the grin was gone.

"Perhaps." He dropped his backpack on the floor. He put a cloth-wrapped package on the counter. "This is for you." He unwrapped it. It contained dried fruit, fresh berries, and freeze-dried cheese. A precious thank you gift, in any case.

"Stay for a while. We'll share it." He smiled at my

words.

We ate slowly, savoring the companionship as much as the food. He took a large portion of cooked onions and potatoes and mint tea after admitting he had not seen either in a long time. It was my turn to smile.

"My name is Jordan."

"Raina." I sipped at the tea. "Talk to me."

"Very well." He spoke of the returning caribou herds and flocks. Brief radio messages of snow in the tropics. Lichen, moss, and mushrooms thriving while conventional crops failed. Humans few and far between, and becoming fewer as their supplies ran out. His tribe survived by hunting as they always had. Their game still survived, and so would they. About two hundred of them were scattered throughout the area. They traced their ancestry back for centuries. Before whites came, time didn't matter.

"Inbred?"

Jordan sighed. "Recessives showed up in a few generations. Then no one wanted to marry us. Christian missionaries passed through but never interfered with our culture even when they left behind bastards. We had no resources to interest industry or agriculture to interest settlers. We were left alone. Mostly still are."

He rose and began to clean up. The fire had burned down, leaving us in near darkness. Yet Jordan moved with ease. He never stumbled or bumped into anything. He tensed suddenly, listening.

"What is it - "

"Shhh." He glided over to my side. "Someone's outside. I'll handle it." He crept out the door, gun in hand. I picked up my dart gun and followed him.

A crescent moon gave scant illumination. A rustle and shift in the shadows set my instincts on edge. Before I could react, a hand covered my mouth. "Silence or your life." A gun pressed against my throat. A sharp knife drew a thin line of blood. "You're human? But he came here -"

"Of course, I'm human. What else -"

"Step away from her." Jordan ordered.

"You should have died when her truck hit you." The sneer was unmistakable.

"Well, I didn't." Jordan was trying to get a clear shot. So was the stranger. And I was in the crossfire.

"Let me go. He -"

"It's not a he! It! It's not human - !"

Jordan fired as the other man did. Jordan spun, fell to his knees, staggered up, and ran towards the shadows. My captor fell back, severely injured. I staggered away from the now limp grip. "Jordan?" Silence. There was a trail of blood. Black blood. Not red like my blood now seeping into my parka collar, or the growing red stain on the ground beneath the dead man. Five paces into the trees plunged me into darkness. "I know you're here."

"Go away."

"You're hurt."

I don't want you to see me this way!" He was huddled against a tree, his back toward me, cradling his left arm. "Go."

"You need help." He tried to scramble away and fell. His green eyes were half-closed, glowing, pupils mere slits. Beneath the hoarse breathing was a light growl. His chest vibrated beneath my hands like a rumbling cat's.

"I knew you were here since ... watched you." Jordan struggled to breathe. Donovan had talked about shadows that didn't seem right, shadows that might have been following him. I'd blamed long paranoid days trying to hunt and coming back empty handed.

"Humans hate us ... try to kill us. With the forever

winter ... we have the advantage for the first time." Another breath. "I told the tribe when you helped me ... to let you live. The man ... I … wouldn't hurt another human ..." Jordan passed out.

The fire was blazing brightly in the fireplace. The mint tea was brewing nicely. The finely chopped cress, tomatoes, onions, and peppers I was stir-frying were almost done. A plate of fresh mushrooms sat on the table. There was a low moan. I placed a cool, damp cloth on his forehead. "Rest."

"Who ..." He tried to focus on my face. "Raina?"

"You shoulder has already healed."

"How long?"

"Two days. How do you feel?"

"I'm alive." He took a sip. You helped me." Another sip. "Dead?"

"Yes."

"You helped me after you knew..." It was a big question wrapped in his statement.

"I made a choice."

"Why me if you had just learned what I was?"

"No one can survive alone."

"Was survival the only factor?"

"No." His green cat-eyes met mine. "You knew where I lived, yet no one ever harmed us except human marauders."

"Yes."

His hand reached out, gingerly, uncertain, and touched mine lightly. An animal, carefully, testing. I knew survival depended on picking the winning side. I squeezed his hand back with forced affection, not letting myself wonder about consequences. "We both know how dangerous humans can be."

BANKING ON HOPE

Don't offer to help unless you know EXACTLY what they're asking for.

BANKING ON HOPE

"I'd like to ask a favor of you."

A dark alley in an unsafe part of town lay outside the window. It was a reminder of a place I shouldn't be ... wouldn't be if I had a choice. "I thought you were dead, Cayet."

"I ..." His eyes flicked to the alley entrance. No one. "I have to lay low."

"What did you do?"

"Nothing! Absolutely nothing!" He lowered his voice. "With the round-ups and identification checks, I can't even risk going to the black market. Besides, they can't even supply what I need. The corporations have stopped producing it, so that leaves just natural sources."

"What do you want me to do?" He whispered his answer softly as if that would make it more palatable. "That's illegal, and you know it! And I don't know anything about manufacturing it, and I'm not going to start trying. Even researching your condition would be a death sentence."

"I'm the one who's under a death sentence. Kenji, please? In all the years we've known each other ... I had you kidnapped just so we could talk. Just to see if you could help."

"I'm being watched because I had been a lab technician for Doctor Dumont for two years. I never participated in that particular project. I don't know how to do what you need done."

"You were there. That might be enough." A sentry flight outside brought all to silence until it passed. "Kenji, I don't have an ident-card any more - but they aren't looking for me either. They mistook one of the others who died when they raided the crèche as me."

"Who did they mistake for you?"

"They counted Reyja and Mallon in the body count, so

no one knows that Mirenjo and I are still alive."

"I don't recognize the names ..." I'd heard of the raids, but no one knew precisely why they had occurred.

"Reyja and Mallon were born four years ago."

My chest turned to ice. The rumors were true. The cause of the riots wasn't a mere rumor. Cayet reiterated what we both knew. "The agreement said the bio-phants could live out their natural span, but no others were to be created. That violated the treaty, so they shut off the supply of the enzyme we need to survive. They programmed that deficiency into our genes deliberately to provide a means of control of what turned out to be a threat. But we refuse to be a biological dead end, just as we refused to live to serve humans."

"What am I supposed to do?"

"All we wanted was citizenship, and the right to use gene therapy to correct the defect."

"Which would have left you independent. But I can't do that. Not my expertise."

"Did they use truth drugs when they interrogated you?"

"One of the hate groups got a hold of me and squeezed me dry. Police got the report."

Pity, revulsion and horror swept over his features. I tried to speak, but he shushed me. Murmuring inanities until the shuddering subsided. He knew how bad interrogations could be. Mirenjo did a blood test, probably to confirm I wasn't still drugged.

"I didn't know ... and they must have hated it when you admitted supporting us." I nodded. The outlaws could do things to me the police could not, and all was tolerated as long as there were no physical scars. I saw Mirenjo's reaction as his portable scanner beeped. It wasn't the familiar tone. Cayet said, "And I'm sorry." Before I could react, I felt the hypospray and the hiss as its contents entered my bloodstream. Then darkness.

I awoke on a cot with Cayet leaning over me. I was groggy from the injection, but that was preferable to the ache in my bones. "Rest, Kenji, it's done."

"Done what?"

"You worked in the lab. You were exposed to the virus that created our deficiencies and caused the disorder that left us dependant on enzymes. You have antibodies to that viral carrier. We now have a sample of that."

"Keeping the next generation from your fate."

"More than that! We've set up a culture from your tissue to produce the enzymes naturally. Like cell cultures producing insulin. But your cultured cells won't be destroyed if the authorities infect it with the virus, which even normal human cells would be. It's enough to support me and three others. I have a chance at survival now. We all do."

I remembered the flu-like symptoms from the mild exposure. A resistant human and vaccinated to boot. I was merely a technician, but I didn't have to be replaced like my predecessors. "Now what?"

"You're safe."

"I can't go home."

"You're right. You can't."

"Then where will I go?"

"We'll keep you safe."

"Your people don't like humans –"

Cayet smiled reassuringly. "You won't be harmed. We need your marrow. We'll need it for a long time and for a lot of our kind. You'll be safe."

DOUBLE TROUBLE

What if all your problems really WERE your father's fault?

DOUBLE TROUBLE

"I need to sue my father."

"On what basis?" The lawyer asked.

"That is where I need a lawyer's advice. Child endangerment? Or reckless endangerment? Child abuse?"

The lawyer took another hard look at his prospective client. The young man appeared in his mid-twenties. Streaks of gray in his jet-black hair made him appear older. The trembling left hand that was kept stiffly to his side hinted about a nervous condition. He was getting tired of spoiled brats trying to sue for their trust funds, but his practice wasn't making enough money to be picky about clients. "I think the statute of limitations would apply, sir."

"What's the statute's limit?"

"7 years from date of last abuse."

"So I would have to have filed within seven years of my birth?" The potential client grimaced. The left corner of his mouth curled up with a sharp spasm as he leaned back in the chair. "Damn." he said.

"I'm sorry." The lawyer apologized as he observed the man's attack. The symptoms looked like Parkinson's, yet the young man didn't seem old enough to suffer from a disease of old age.

"Were you a victim of flawed genetic engineering? In that basis, we could sue the doctor for medical malpractice. Or, if your parents' contract prevents them from suing, you could at least sue for medical neglect." The lawyer tried to keep his tone optimistic but not eager. "Am I to assume your medical condition relates to the manner of your conception?"

"Yes."

"Then we can sue the doctor, if not your parents."

"Do you have to be a legal adult to do that?"

"Yes."

"What is that age?"

"21. Unless legally emancipated at an earlier -"

"Then I'll have to be emancipated."

"Exactly how old are you?"

"17. But I finished my GED two years ago. I finished a college degree a few weeks ago."

"Educational achievement is not enough for adult status."

"I'm not self-supporting, but I do have a trust fund."

"Is it in your name?"

"When I am considered a legal adult."

"That is four more years."

"I don't think I have that long."

The lawyer leaned back in his chair. Terminal illness caused by a lousy genetic enhancement procedure? That was a strong suit against the doctor. Why wouldn't the parents sue in the minor's name? It could be that a legal contract prevented such. Or perhaps the fear that the lawsuit would make public the knowledge that they had tried to enhance their own child, with all the social repercussions and legal consequences it could bring was stopping them. Why sue the parents? Resentment against the parents, perhaps? The son was blaming them for his suffering and wanted to make them suffer in return rather than the more profitable party.

"I could fill out the forms to have you emancipated. We could then sue the doctors for medical neglect. If the genetic enhancement procedure was done in a country outside jurisdiction, we could still threaten legal charges and seek a settlement."

"I want to sue my father."

"If you sue your parents, your mother would have to be included."

"I only have one biological parent. My father. He hired a surrogate to bear me."

The stories of men who had children via donated eggs and hired wombs had started to circulate. "We could sue the egg supplier for inferior goods."

"The donated egg was fine. It was my father's DNA that was the problem."

"He had an inherited disorder that was passed on?"

"The problem is related to *how* I was conceived."

"Now we're back to suing the doctors again."

The client put his head in his hands. His fingers brushed up against his graying streak, spasming as they did, as if he'd rip out the offending hairs on impulse. His voice was low as the next words tumbled out. "I'm a clone."

The lawyer dropped his electronic notepad onto the desk but hardly heard the clatter. "That's illegal!" He quickly and carefully made certain it was still in record mode. "*You* are illegal."

"I know."

"I don't even know if you could file a suit. You have no legal standing."

"I have a birth certificate. I have a home-schooling record. I have a college degree."

"But you're not legally human. It was the only way the government could reconcile the public repulsion against cloning and the right to replicate as one chooses. The government couldn't stop people from going overseas and having children created. All it could do was denying them legal status. Doing so meant the government could not be held liable for the potential medical costs if there were health problems related to the cloning. It also partially satisfied the moralists." The young man's physical spasms took on an unnerving dimension. "How old are you?"

"Chronologically, 17. Biologically, 22. Genetically, 67."

"Is the … health condition related to the cloning?"

"Parkinson's is kicking in due to my genetic age."

"Parkinson's isn't fatal."

"All the other symptoms of old age will show up soon."

"That is why you want to sue him in particular. To punish him."

"Yes."

"The ramifications were only theoretical then."

"If cloned animals died young of old age, why shouldn't someone be held liable for ignoring the consequences if they did it in humans?"

"There was no certainty that the same would hold true for humans. Especially given the effort to correct the problem. It is like the health warning on prescription drugs. If you use the medical alternatives, you are accepting the possible side effects. Your condition, I am sad to say, is a likely side effect." The lawyer picked his pad up off the floor and made certain it was in record mode. "I'm sorry."

"So I can't sue until I'm 21?"

"I couldn't ever help you. You have no legal standing."

"I was conceived in Mexico, but I was born in Laredo, Texas. That makes me American. I'll make my legal stand under the law, even if I have to wait until I'm old enough."

"You are American only on your birth certificate. Once it is known that you are a clone, you will not have any legal rights."

"Not even when I'm old enough?"

"You weren't legally human when you were manufactured, much less now."

"Can you prosecute him for creating me?"

"Yes."

"And sue him for wrongful birth?"

"The courts have never recognized wrongful birth."

"Wrongful conception?"

"Wrongfully conceived equals should have been aborted. You weren't aborted."

"Yeah, I'm here."

"And you're here." The lawyer checked the recording time left on his device. He still had plenty of time. He'd be able to protect himself from any legal repercussions. "Does your … father know where you are?"

"He just knows that I'm out."

"What does he think you're doing?"

"Looking for a graduate school to go to."

"Have you actually been admitted to a school?"

"Yeah. To the state college in town."

The lawyer felt a smile. "How did you get in?"

"My father gave them a large enough donation that they didn't look too hard at my DNA signature."

"All ID cards are based on DNA."

"My ID says 'Mexican', reflecting my birth mother's background. So my DNA profile is checked against the Mexican national database instead of the American one. The match between my father's and mine doesn't show up that way."

"Clever." It was an admirable attempt to circumvent the law. He might have even thought of it himself. "But that's risky." Time for the disclaimer, the lawyer thought. "It is also illegal. ID manipulation always involves jail time."

"It doesn't matter anyway. I probably won't live to finish a real degree."

"I'll report your father to the authorities." *And collect the reward involved for turning in the criminals ...* "Can I use this conversation as evidence?"

"I guess."

"Is that a yes?" It had to be a definite yes, or it wouldn't be admissible in court.

"Yes. You can use my words to send him to jail."

"You'll have to answer some legal questions."

"That's what *your* job is."

More than you know. "Can you tell me more about your doctor?"

"The Parkinson's doctor?"

"No, no. The one who helped clone you." The lawyer felt brief sympathy for the clone. He'd die in medical isolation before long ... the clone was an innocent injured party. He made a mental note to seek medical treatment for the young man in exchange for his testimony. Not legal immunity, since that couldn't exist for the illegally born. But perhaps better treatment and home confinement rather than a jail cell. The kid shouldn't suffer more in his quest for justice ...

The lawyer pushed his emotions aside. If he had the details to prosecute the doctors who had cloned the father, he could seek to join the prosecution team when they went after the geneticists. It would be a high profile case. It would be profitable. Even if only a few arrests were made, the reward money would certainly pick up his slow practice. "Do you remember much about them?"

THE HUNTER AND THE HUNTER

Better ability doesn't make for better people.

THE HUNTER AND THE HUNTED

Someone was in pain.

Lorraine stopped mid-stride and rocked back onto her heels at the sensation. Her eyes swept across the street to see what had triggered the unusual event. The streets were empty but for a few scattered souls. The muddled thoughts of those typically wandering this time of night were from the myriad intoxicants they had consumed. The only clear mind in sight was an annoyed cop waiting three blocks over to catch a jerk he'd been waiting to bust for weeks. Neon signs flashed against a cloudy midnight sky, almost as bright as Officer Mendoza's mind.

She flashed images of everyone she had ever cared for through her mind. The images didn't trigger anything specific, so she knew that the pain was not that of someone that mattered to her. That left only the possibility of someone very close by, and in intense pain.

Lorraine started walking straight ahead as she let her barriers down again. The pain grew stronger. She turned the corner. It grew weaker. She backtracked. She closed her mind again to focus on the visual world. Then she saw the alley.

Lorraine stepped soundlessly into the shadows. The loud broadcast of pain stopped abruptly. It was as if whomever was broadcasting had heard her approach. The only person present was a man sitting against the wall. His knees were drawn to his chest and his head in his arms. He didn't move.

"Are you alright?" Lorraine asked. Had one of the homeless fools injured himself again? Turning him over to authorities would improve her Good Samaritan image, and keep the cops away from her for another few months.

No response. She strode up to the man, and then she knelt beside him. She felt for his pulse; it was slow, but strong.

Was he unconscious? Lorraine emptied her mind of stray thoughts and focused on the stranger. She sensed nothing from him. That in itself was puzzling. The unconscious, at least, broadcast a life-sign. The drunk or drugged radiated a jumble of emotions that was sheer chaos. Only the dead felt so empty. But he wasn't dead!

A sharp wave of criticism and disgust hit Lorraine. She looked up to see why, and saw a middle-aged woman watching them. Lorraine read the woman's mind. The older woman thought that Lorraine and the stranger were a pair, and shook her head at the pitiful sight of them. Lorraine only glared back, keeping her face neutral. The older woman left, shaking her head.

Lorraine focused her attention back onto the stranger. She sensed a change of some sort. Something had given or shifted. Then it hit her. A mind - block! She couldn't recognize it at first because it had been so long since she'd sensed one. No one except another telepath would be able to mind - block.... And the Pogroms led by the authorities were hunting down and killing those like her.

Lorraine focused her thoughts: *Can you hear this?*

The stranger started. His head jerked up and his eyes met hers. His hand rose halfway to her face, paused, and then touched her cheek. The mind block dropped with the physical contact. A rich baritone drawl filled her mind. *Yes, I ... can. Can you?* His eyes begged for a response. Waves of emotion flowed with the contact. Lorraine had to shut down the contact to prevent the overload.

Lorraine nodded. It was then that she noticed the scent of alcohol on his breath and clothes. The desperation in his eyes was too much to stand. A notion formed in her mind. She said: *Come with me.*

He rose shakily to his feet.

The stranger passed out as soon as he hit the couch. As unconsciousness settled on the man, the mind - block dropped. She could sense his endlessly shifting dreams, but not his memories. Habit or something stronger kept her from probing his mind any further. She let him be.

It wasn't until that moment that the import of what she had done hit her. She had brought a total stranger - and a telepath, at that - to her apartment in the middle of the night. She never let anyone into her place. Ever. All reason and logic said that this was a very, very bad idea. Instinctively, though, it felt right.

She eased his boots, jacket and shirt off. He didn't stir. She went into her own bedroom and lay down on the bed. After a moment's indecision, she locked the door.

Lorraine woke irritable, but she could not determine why. Lorraine began to fix breakfast. She kept one mental ear on her visitor and another on Mrs. Nieman. Lorraine sensed the woman's bright satisfaction when Li gave her the money back when she made her morning run to the store.

Kail came to in someone else's apartment. He felt well enough with only a mild headache, which was surprising in itself. The wild kaleidoscope of humanity in the space around him was just far enough away for the real world to catch up with him. He saw his shirt, reached for it, leaned too far, and hit the floor. That woke him up the rest of the way.

Before he buttoned it, he smelled fresh food cooking. Had he been so locked on the mental blocks that he'd forgotten such a basic sense as smell? A young woman was stir-frying an omelet. She glanced up from the pan, scooped half the omelet onto a plate, and gave him the plate. Kail's jaw dropped. It was not his favorite food, but certainly one of his preferences. A light soprano voice filled his mind. *Yes. It's for you.* The blur of the prior night refused to come into focus. Just what had he done?

Kail wolfed down the food. He couldn't sense her thoughts, but he couldn't be sure he hadn't manipulated her into caring for him. Or had it been something else, managing to come home with someone after the fiasco at the bar? The woman paused in her own eating with her fork halfway to her mouth. The soprano voice began in his mind. *Do you like it?*

Kail couldn't believe that her thoughts could come through so clearly. Was he out of practice, or was she unusually strong? He asked her. Another possibility occurred to him. *Why are you doing this?*

Why did you ask for help if you didn't want it? Her mental tone was indignant.

She was a telepath like him. He kept eating and reinforced any route she would have had into his mind. *When did I ask for help?*

Kail could tell she was angry from her expression, though he could not sense the emotion. How was she able to transmit her thoughts so clearly if he couldn't receive clearly? If he could hear her clearly, could she read him despite his blocks? How would he get out of this? What was the best tactic? Honesty is the best policy, he decided, this time at least. Tell her the truth.

The city has so many minds in such a small area. I missed the bus out of town. I had nowhere to go, no way to block out all of the emotions, the needs, the fears. Under too much stress, my control faltered. The only way to block the minds out was to meditate or pass out. And the fastest, easiest way was to get drunk. She didn't need to know what had caused the stress.

Lorraine listened to his "speech". She knew information was lacking, but didn't press. *I agree. It is often hard to block.*

Lorraine jumped reflexively as he surged forward into her mind. Hung over or not, he was still in control. It was a serious breach of the social protocols that had begun developing before the crackdowns on their kind. He caught himself at the sight of her physical reaction. The mental block went up and the assault stopped.

Lorraine was outraged. Was it possible he'd even manipulated her while drunk, supposedly harmless? *Get out!*

Kail pushed himself back. *Listen. I'm not forcing you right now. I swear -*

Lorraine was on her feet. Manipulations, indeed! *Get out! Get out of my apartment! Get out of my mind!*

Kail stepped towards her. He was too close for comfort. Lorraine had known of other psychics, but she had done what she could so that they never knew that she was one of them. She obviously couldn't hide the fact that she was a telepath to him. He already knew. But she could -

She lunged for the phone. He reached it first and tore it off the wall. She threw up mental barriers even as he tried to tear them down. A darkness fell in Lorraine s' mind, a protective reflex against the overload.

Lorraine woke bound and gagged on the couch. A brief groggy moment and she knew she was still home. No, not home. Just in her apartment. Kail was sitting across from her on the floor. His rich baritone echoed in her mind. *You did catch me at a bad time, but I am ... sober now. Ah, you have figured out why I am here. It is incredibly easy to manipulate the average human, though it is much harder to influence a psychic -*

Lorraine threw her rage at him. His mind block went up; the attack had no effect. She went passive again. "That is the attitude that started the Pogroms."

\- *Anyway. I agree with the idea. Of the Pogroms. I*

could not afford having any rivals, but what use is it to be alone? I want more than just living my life. You are the last one left, and you were one of the best. I realized that when it took so long to track you down.

- *You hid so well from your own kind that none of them could tell authorities where you were; hence you escaped the rounds of psychics turning each other in to buy themselves more time. And you were skillful enough to hide in plain sight even as others of our kind fell apart. You were not even suspected of being ... unusual. Only the few ghosts of a memory that I could scan at a safe distance, of course - implied that you still existed.*

- *You had no ambition. You had no grand dreams of any kind. You had no entangling attachments to anyone of either kind. That made you the exception of our kind. That was the one thing anyone remembered about you, the nagging suspicion of your talent. Once nearby, I was certain.*

So go do as you please, Lorraine offered.

You would still be a threat to me if left alone. You disagree with me on the nature of the world and how it should be. I can't risk a confrontation. Yet there are options.

Lorraine began to fight the bonds. They were too tight. "How so?"

Kail was amused that she chose to only speak to him now. He continued: *I beat all of the others; either by tip-offs or basically outlasting them. All dead, but one. All but you. I give you a choice.* He leaned forward and his hand fell to her throat. *You can be my means of genetic immortality or ...* The hand on her throat tightened.

Her eyes narrowed. *Will you kill any children with a psychic talent, too?*

Kail sighed. *Any but my own. Any mundane people in the population carrying the gene that results in us are dead or sterilized because of the Pogroms. Only psychics now can have psychic children. And we are the last psychics left.*

He touched her face, and then pulled back as she hit him with her fury. Kail continued: *I can force thoughts into other people's minds. I could do so with you. I could make you ... feel the way I want you to. It could be fun. It could be painful. I could lock you into any delusion I want. Or that you want. I don't have to do that. Your choice, Lorraine?*

Lorraine concentrated on the bindings. They loosened an infinitesimal amount. She finally responded in kind, forcing her emotional turmoil so the shame and pity came to the forefront to hide the other emotions and her thoughts: *Kail?*

Kail's smiling eyes met hers. *Yes?*

She kept her face expressionless so that she didn't have to concentrate on three things at once. She continued: *Before you make plans of dominating me, there is something you should know.*

His expression brightened with amusement. He leaned forward, his mind scanning other aspects. He was trying to determine if she were already pregnant. *What is it?*

"Things are not always what they seem." The bindings loosened and fell off her wrists and ankles. The gag that had been in her mouth fell to the floor. Within seconds, Kail was thrown from his sitting position on the floor up to the ceiling. The impact didn't cause enough brain damage, so she threw him onto the floor.

"Kail, I have to admit something. It's true that I have no such plans, but you are not the best. I was hiding something else. Another talent." Kail felt a gossamer touch on his throat that mimicked a human hand. She continued, "I may not be able to force thoughts into other people's minds like you did to me, but telekinesis is ample consolation for being unique in the world."

The gossamer touch became a tight grip on his throat.

"I'm equally outcast as a psychic in the mundane world as I knew I would be among psychics for this ability. I have no home. My best option was to watch as the weak got rounded up and the strong killed each other. I alone would remain." Kail was turning blue from the ghost hands on his throat. "It is not that I had no ambition. I did have an ambition – to survive. That is, and must always be, the foremost goal."

She waited until his brain stopped before letting go. Although she had never touched him, she spent hours in the shower.

Lorraine allowed herself to float about a meter above the bed. She reached into the computer and set it working on the proper calculations for her latest freelance data-modeling job. Another touch and it sped up the number crunching until the computer glowed with the heat. She'd have the work done in a tenth the time. She was paid so well for her occasional assignments that she never needed to bother with the hassle of a regular job.

Why had no one else bothered to work on such applications of their abilities? Were they so busy dominating average folk and each other that they never wondered what else they could do? She let her mind brush the keyboard, e-mailing the results to the firm that paid her this week.

Kail stirred on the other side of the room. Lorraine settled back onto the bed. She floated Kail another meter away from her so that he was pressed against the wall. "It's about time you woke up."

Kail blinked against the sunlight streaming through the window. He reached for his throat. "What have you done?"

"What do you think I 've done?"

"Gotten even." Kail tried to muster rage but failed; he was too drained. "What have you done to me?"

"I did a little improving."

"Improving?" he croaked. There was a note of fear in his mind.

"You lacked a conscience. I gave you one. It was that or kill you."

"I can't sense you."

"Only other psychics are a threat. You are no longer a threat." The oxygen deprivation would have been enough to kill the talent if she hadn't intentionally rewritten that portion of his brain.

The full import of her words didn't reach him. "You almost killed me!" He only cared about the strangling.

"I can't work on a conscious mind."

"I would rather be dead than changed."

Lorraine dropped her mental barrier, waiting, keeping her thoughts nil so that he wouldn't know what she expected. He felt for the part of her mind where her second talent laid, a low-level telekinesis ability he lacked, but could manipulate via his own telepathy. As he immediately reached for it, the trigger Lorraine had created inside his mind went off. Everything Kail was and had ever been vanished.

"I told you, I gave you a conscience." She stared down at the breathing shell of the man. "And conscience requires consequences for your own actions." She wished she hadn't had to do it. Then again, it was either implanting a fatal feed back loop in his mind to kill him if he tried to harm her, or she getting killed. He would have been fine if he hadn't tried to hurt her again. But that was not his nature. There was no blood on her hands.

She'd have to fake his entry and hit him with something in the head – something other than telepathy to explain his comatose state. She'd then have to pull out in a hurry, complaining profusely about the lack of safety in the neighborhood. She could make some deals and sell everything in a few hours. She'd be out before the autopsy showed what he was, much less any possible blame on her. She would disappear again.

At least this would be the last time.

THE GHOSTS OF TEDJAI

Ghosts come in all forms, and on all worlds.

THE GHOSTS OF TEDJAI

A stranger dressed in furs and denim entered the store with a string of gutted rabbits tossed over his shoulder. A young boy dressed only in furs was in step behind him. "Hello." Marcus Halloran offered. There were only half a dozen people in the trading post, all taking in the sight of new faces. Marcus grinned, eager at the possibility of new customers.

"I've come to trade." The stranger's accent was unidentifiable but not impenetrable. He laid the rabbits out on the counter.

"What do you want?"

"Jeans for my son. Tablets of paper. A bolt of cloth, if you have it."

"You have enough here for all that." Lynnette's two young daughters had come out at the sound of unfamiliar voices. They were staring at the child. I could understand why. The boy's hair was gray and his skin was a tawny color; nothing like the "father". Then again, the child's yellow eyes hinted at a mutation, which would explain everything. The boy stared off into the distance, staying close to the father. Was this his first time in civilized society, as small as the trading post was?

The stranger laid the pants out on the counter. Perhaps to reassure Marcus, the stranger took off his fur gloves as he pocketed the pads of paper. You could see it in Marcus' eyes: one, two, three, four fingers and thumb. The father, at least, wasn't a mutant. I noticed heavy scars along the sides of both hands, on both the father and son. They were almost surgical in nature.

Marcus and the strangers concluded the rest of the trade in silence.

I took the ten-kilo bag of hydroponic rice from the supply depot. The rice ration was a fifth what it used to be. After the strangers left, I purchased a few aging cans of vegetables with the last of my pay. It was a cruel irony for a colony founded by would-be farmers.

Everyone knew living here would be hard, just not this hard. Outdoor crops began failing from assaults by alien pests. The greenhouses failed as native mold fouled up water lines. We never thought it would get this bad.

My parents stopped going into Touchdown Town when the food riots started. They stopped going to the trading post when the rations were too small to justify the risk of the trip. Father started hunting; hence, we survived. For those of us like my brother, sister, and self, Earth was more myth than real. The "Tedjai Ghosts" were much more real. The torn up equipment and lost snare lines were testament to their existence.

We eventually discovered what we initially thought was the cause of all our equipment problems. The "Tedjai Ghosts" were creatures similar to small chimps. They weighed about 12 kilos. The critters were omnivores, smart as a two-year-old child, and six-fingered like all other Tedjai mammals. They liked to play with metal, and tore wires apart with avid curiosity. We had our answer.

There were sightings of larger creatures. The McRae family began electrifying their traps to scare the beasts away. A few weeks later, his traps were found with the battery wires meticulously disconnected and the hinges destroyed. The prey were not only gone, but the only means Ailun McCrae had of catching meat for his family had been destroyed. Ailun set up a hidden camera to watch the next batch of traps. He couldn't afford the electronics, but he could less afford to let his family starve.

McCrae was furious when the recordings showed a blurry someone deliberately opening the trap and removing his catch. He couldn't identify whom; the electronics were too cheap, the image too poor.

The next time his traps went out, he went out too with a rifle. There were no skimmer tracks. Yet he couldn't rule out the idea someone hiking all that way to steal from him, this was during the hungry years. He waited for the perpetrator to come back. Two nights later, it did.

One of the town doctors was asked to do an autopsy on what was left after Ailun was done venting his anger. What was left looked like a cousin to the little primates. It had six digits per hand and the digestive system of a native species. It was probably male. No one could be completely certain, although biology between the two worlds were only slightly different from each other. The dead thing was either a bigger cousin of the little primates, or a big mutated primate.

Everyone became wary after the doctor's verdict. A chimp could rip an arm off of a human. If this cousin primate was as large as a human, how strong was it? How smart? McCrae's traps weren't the only ones being raided either. Eventually, McCrae's family starved. McRae himself didn't starve; his body was found bludgeoned to death.

My father had been the one to find McCrae dead, while hunting between the two homesteads. Upon the discovery, he went to the McCrae homestead to inform the men still there. McRae's nephew, and two young men from town, who wanted to learn hunting from McRae, were dead. None of their food was stolen. None of their weapons were taken. The items used to bludgeon them to death were never found. Thus started the more frightening version of the myth of Tedjai's Ghosts.

People would shoot at shadows, sometimes killing people by accident when they did. If they thought they killed a "ghost", it was gone before anyone got to where the body should have been. The fear drove many people back to town and off the planet. Those that stayed died from other causes.

Tedjai's native fevers killed half the population the year after McCrae's murder. Those born on Earth either died or purged the alien diseases completely from their system. However, those born here who survived the fevers did so with the native bacterium living in their systems afterward. The threat of epidemic loomed over us all from that day forward. The isolation of quarantine sank in as Earth forbade ships from visiting our world. Soon, no one could leave, and no one came. No sane captain would bring people to our deathtrap of a world. We were alone. Except for Tedjai's Ghosts.

"Renada!" The sound of my name brought me to a halt and back to reality. Kelly caught up with me as I walked back toward my skimmer. "I didn't know you were here."

"I'm just picking up supplies." A storm was brewing over the mountains, but I wanted to talk to her. There were so few people left, and even fewer that I could call friend. Yet ice was already frosting the treetops at the higher elevations. It was time to go home if I wanted to make it home. I gave her a wane smile and carried the groceries to my skimmer. I raced over the permafrost towards home.

If I went to town to join the few hundred people who still lived there, I'd feel a false security of safely in numbers. However, long-term survival meant surviving the on Tedjai as it truly was, in its raw form, out here in the wilderness. The first colonists sought to make it in Earth's image. Tedjai's native life had fought back in a primitive manner, killing many. If we survived a few more generations, we might be as much a part of Tedjai as Homo Sapiens had been of Earth. But we'd have to survive first.

Surviving as a people – and keeping our humanity in the process – meant forging a truce between all the Ghosts of Tedjai. Those broken dreams whose aftermath still shaped our lives, the ghosts of all those who died here, and whatever native creatures wandered these forbidding woods. I told myself that as I kept pushing the old skimmer on the trail home. It meant getting along with the living, too. Even if that meant getting along with the rudest of humans, like Marcus Halloran.

Alex and I met the next week in Lynnette's "restaurant" the next month to discuss the native wildlife. Lynette provided the table, food, and service; hence, a restaurant. The stranger was back and talking to Lynnette. I hardly paid attention to Alex. Alex was chatting about my notes. My "field reports" of native plants and animals were the only income source I had. One couldn't live off the standard rations anymore. So I pretended to listen to him in order to keep my "job".

I kept trying not to stare at the golden-eyed child. He was wearing the jeans from his last visit. He looked like it was the first time he'd ever worn them, since he kept shifting and pulling at them. He showed no curiosity about Marcus' two nieces, though the girls kept staring at him. Was his family so isolated that he had neither knowledge nor interest in other people? I pitied the boy.

Finally, Alex said, "Keep up the good work." We shook hands. He paid me as he took my hand written notes. He was returning to town to a warm, secure office. Alex had become acquainted with me through letters I sent to town asking questions only a scientist could answer. Before then, he hadn't thought anyone of any intelligence lived out here. I gave him information he wasn't willing to gather himself. Alex didn't notice the stranger and Marcus in an argument. Marcus and the stranger's argument was getting heated. Someone needed to intervene. "Is anything wrong?" I asked.

Marcus answered, "I asked for ID."

"I can pay with food later."

"What does he want?" I asked.

"He wants a couple kilos of that red and gray fungus. But he can't pay for it. He wants to pay me back *later* in meat."

The stranger tensed slightly. "I'll go elsewhere if you don't agree to my terms."

"What elsewhere?" Marcus challenged.

"I'll pay for it, if you must have cash." I held out the pay from Alex.

"Renada, why -?"

The stranger said, "No."

"You'll throw away an act of generosity like that? Idiot." Marcus grinned. "What are you afraid of? No name. No ID. What are you hiding? Maybe you killed somebody in town?" I wanted to curse out loud at Marcus.

"Or, maybe, you're such a freak you couldn't register as a person -" A fist caught Marcus square in the chest. Marcus pulled out a knife and sliced randomly in the stranger's direction as he tried to get air.

The stranger moved like lightening and could have easily fled, but he refused to leave the fight. I tried to pull the boy away from the two men, but he shied away from me. Lynette pulled her two daughters into a back room. Marcus got his wind back and got in closer. The stranger missed Marcus with a few swings and grazed him with others. Marcus had been a bully in school, and it showed. He wasn't vicious, just vengeful. The stranger had struck first, and Marcus wasn't going to let that go. Neither man stopped until Marcus landed his blade into the other man's flesh.

A low, soft sound came from the stranger as he finally staggered back. The stranger pressed his arm against the gash. The layers of clothing he wore seemed to be soaking up his blood. The stranger shivered once. Then he leaned on his son and staggered out the door.

"You *idiot*!" Shopkeeper or not, the man who controlled whether or not I got my rations or not, I couldn't keep my silence. "What are you trying to do? "

"He was acting funny around my nieces." The man's arrogant green eyes met mine. If he weren't the owner of the trading post, no one would tolerate his behavior.

I stormed out. I watched the stranger and child get on their skimmer and race off. Everyone who lived out here suspected any stranger of being a Tedjai Ghost. We guessed that anyone we didn't know might be one. It was the only explanation we had for why we'd never seen one. How they had learned English or to act like us, was anyone's guess. Whether a fugitive's child or a mutant, it wouldn't be right to risk the child being left alone if the man bled to death from Marcus' attack.

I found the pair an hour later by following the skimmer's tracks. The man was half-curled up on the ground. The snow around him was a faded orange. I wanted to gag from the stink. Orange blood! Only native creatures had orange blood. He was Tedjai! Oh, Lord, the rumors were true - Tedjai could pass for human.

The boy was watching me with those bright yellow eyes. What was he?

"How badly is he hurt?" No response. How much English did he know? His father was breathing unevenly. Unconscious? "Will you come with me? " No response. "I have medical supplies at home. " The boy let me ease his father onto my skimmer. I was able to tie the Tedjai's skimmer to mine. The boy got onto his craft and stayed there. He held on for dear life before I even got my craft started.

It was the longest ride home in my life. I didn't let myself think of the possible consequences for my actions. All I could think of was of another needless death. Death had taken too many people away from me already.

My mother died of complications from a miscarriage, because help was too far away. My brother had found our father frozen to death, clutching a knife to his chest against whatever might come out of the shadows, while he lay in the snow with a broken leg. My brother and sister were nearly grown at the time. Our brother was mobile enough and fair enough at hunting to keep the three of us fed. However, it had been terrifying and difficult. With our parents dead we dared not venture out farther than necessary. Neighbors, who feared a fever had killed us all, were too afraid check on us for over a year. I couldn't leave a child in far worse circumstances than those my family barely survived.

Finally, home. I dragged the stranger inside. I carefully undressed the man as best I could. From the outside, he looked human. I focused on the wound. The knife had cut into muscles on the chest. An inhuman network of sinew was exposed by the gash. I put old pressure bandages on the wound. The antibiotics lay where they were; I didn't know if they'd do any good. The bleeding finally stopped. An orange mess covered the floor of my living room. The large one was still unconscious, but he might not bleed to death now. It was the best I could do.

Now, for the child .. "Do you have a name?" Silence. "Are you hungry?" Nothing. "My name is Renada Dumont." His eyes followed me as I pulled out a plate of native fungi from the refrigerator. He nibbled at the food after he'd taken refuge in a corner near the adult.

Strange dreams haunted me. My brother Levin told me often that if I did not behave, the Tedjai Ghosts would take me away into the forest. I yelled back that maybe they would, but only after punishing him for saying such mean things. The child's face filled my mind's eye; had the Tedjai taken him away from his family to enable the "father" to pass as human? Was the Tedjai here to take me away?

When Levin had died two years prior, he'd screamed that he saw them, horrible ruby red eyes gleaming. I tried to talk sense into him as I tried to pour herbal potions down his throat. He saw me, but he didn't recognize me. He certainly didn't hear me. Our sister had fallen into a coma within a day of developing a fever. She hadn't had a chance and died within a week. Levin had fought it for weeks. He fought it so long that I thought he might even have made a recovery. Yet, despite all my efforts, he still died. For reasons I couldn't fathom, I never got sick. I wondered which of the three of us was the lucky one. I bolted upright, drenched in sweat. Oh, God, what had I done?

Perhaps it was a show of trust that the boy never came at me with a knife. Or was that only after the man recovered? I spoke to him often, to gauge for his reactions, to test his understanding, to fill in the silence. Since I'd just made a supply run, no one would think to check on me for a long time. I was completely on my own.

The portraits of my family stared down on the strange affair. I saw the child glance up at them from time to time. Had he never seen pictures? "Good morning." The boy peeked around a doorway at my words. "Are you hungry?" He watched me fix my own breakfast. "Do you want meat?" I tossed a piece of rabbit on the counter. He didn't touch it. "If I let you outside, will you catch something to eat? Or will you fetch another Tedjai? " He froze when I opened the door. I closed it again. It was too cold out to wait for the child to maybe make a decision.

I tried reading to him from old children's books. I didn't know if he understood, or even if he cared. But it passed the time. I fell asleep that evening while reading. When I awoke in the middle of the night, he was gone. Shortly before morning, I saw him dismembering a native rodent with a stone knife. I closed my eyes. He was eating and it wasn't me. That was progress.

In the early morning, I opened the door to look out. Three more native rodents were on the front step, necks broken. The boy pulled out another storybook and held it out to me, hands stained from the orange blood of his breakfast. He had just eaten meat no human could eat. Hence, he wasn't human. Part of me wanted to see an innocent child. Part of me wanted to not touch a book an alien was holding. I took the book and started reading. The blood stains irritated my skin, but I didn't stop.

Morning brought progress. The adult was awake before I was. Native rodent bones were piled in my fireplace. The adult stared at me unblinkingly and asked, "Why did you help?"

"Marcus shouldn't have hurt you."

"Why did you help after you knew I was ... not like you?"

"I was curious."

"Too curious."

"How did your people learn English?"

"From hunters."

"Are those hunters still alive?" I'd known too many who'd disappeared not to ask.

"No." The very faint glimmer of hope faded as quietly as it had arrived.

"Did you kill them?"

"Not me. Some of them died of disease." Was he trying to be conciliatory?

It wasn't best to be talking about dead humans. "Why come to the trading post?"

"I trade rabbit meat you eat for fungus we eat. It is easier than us trying to gather it, and less fighting if you don't hunt on our land."

"Where is your land?"

"It is all our land."

Time to change directions again. "How long have your people been passing as human?"

"When we can."

I was running out of things to ask, and wondering how long he'd tolerate me asking. "Your diseases kill our people. Do our diseases kill your people?"

"Yes."

"What is your name?"

"Teekan."

"What is the boy's name?"

"Amari."

"Did he tell you my name?"

"Renada Dumont." So the child did understand a little English. "Why did the man -?" Teekan gestured the blade's path.

"He said you acted strangely towards his nieces, towards his sister's two daughters. The two blonde girls with the purple eyes." Marcus was proud to be utterly normal, but that perfection didn't extend to the rest of his bloodline. "He was afraid you would hurt them." I was guessing, but I wanted to make the man's act seem reasonable.

" The smaller one ... touched me."

"Your people don't like to be touched?"

"Not by humans."

Some corner of my mind noted that this was probably the longest conversation anyone had had with one of them and lived. "Are you going to kill Marcus?"

"No."

"Are you going to hurt him?"

"No."

"Your people have killed humans. We've killed your people." Directly, maybe, indirectly, yes. "If you kill Marcus, other humans will kill you. Then we will start killing each other again. If you don't kill Marcus, other people won't have to die."

"I will not kill him, Marcus."

"Will someone else kill Marcus?" Part of me wanted to make sure he understood the "No one kill Marcus" point (Or, perhaps, only the "don't kill more humans" idea).

"No."

We stared at each other in silence. I wanted to ask him a more hundred questions. "Are there any other questions you want to ask me?"

"No."

"You can leave, if you want." Stupid thing to say, Renada. You can't keep him here. Nor would you want to force him. "Or you could stay longer," I offered.

Teekan began adjusting clothing. A soft growl brought Amari to his side. He tugged at Amari's furs until it more resembled a parka. Dressed only in furs now, they looked a little alike.

"How did you learn English?"

"A child."

"How did you learn English as a child?" No answer. "Is Amari your child?"

"Yes."

"Where is his mother?"

"Dead."

"How did she die?"

"Of your diseases." There was what might have been a scowl on his face. I wanted to think it was grief. However, parallel evolution or not, it was best not to make assumptions.

"I'm sorry."

"Sorry?" Teekan chuffed softly. The child's cheeks and throat puffed eerily in response.

"How long ago?"

His nostrils flared wide, wider than humanly possible. "Human time does not matter."

"My parents have died. My siblings have died. That was a long time –"

"I know they are dead."

Had he been watching me? Or word of mouth? It might not be wise to ask. "We may not understand much about each other, but I do understand loss."

"Loss."

I guessed it was a question. "Loss. Death. When people leave and don't come back. It is when they become ghosts."

"We are leaving." He opened the door for himself, not bothering to wait for me to get it. I could barely keep up with him.

"Can you find your way home?"

Teekan's eyes flickered. It might have been a rapidly blurred blink. "I do not get lost like humans."

"I've never gotten lost." Almost never, there'd been a few panicky moments out in the woods. "I've lived here my whole life."

"Humans are lost." The way he said it seemed so cryptic. Did he mean all humans get lost eventually? Did he mean we all die too soon? Or did he know what a lost cause was?

"We will become ghosts." Teekan was a few steps beyond the door when he said it, and he stopped mid-stride. Amari stared up at him, looking very confused. "We are not ghosts like she."

Teekan checked his skimmer carefully before they raced away. He never said another word. Neither did the child. Teekan never clarified who the ghost was. The child's mother? Me? He'd answered far more questions that I'd dared hoped. Yet I was left with more questions.

Had someone been so desperate for human companionship, that they'd ignored the signs who the Tedjai were, and taught them human technology? Maybe if they'd left a helpless, speechless child left on the doorstep like Amari … I would have. After learning about us, the child could then go home and teach others what it had learned. Maybe that was why Amari was brought along.

When I went back inside, the alien scent filled the air. It lingered like musk, filling the air. The smell from the orange bloodstain on the floor might make me nauseous with time. Thinking about what had happened already did.

I'd talked to a Tedjai. The Tedjai was able to talk to me. We'd been talking to Tedjai face to face for who knew how long. They were real. They'd really been here. It was too much to absorb at once.

My sister's picture was staring down at me, bright red eyes smiling. My own silver eyes had attracted less derision than hers. Our brother had been normal, but for his misshapen leg. A Tedjai wouldn't stand out very much among the humans out here in the wilds. Just one more member of the odd, Tedjai-born family.

I collapsed onto the floor, still staring at her. I closed my eyes and let my head rest against the hearthstone. The fire crackled and sighed as it devoured the last of the alien bones. "I guess you're the only ghost left in the house now, sister."

MOMENT OF HUMANITY

Humanity's children will only survive if they can find something in common.

MOMENT OF HUMANITY

"Get down!"

My reaction was fast enough for me to survive the first blast. The ground jumped up to hit us a split second after the explosion. Dust clogged the air. Hot wind blasted across the now broken concrete and twisted shards of steel.

"Scatter and regroup!"

The orders were barely audible above the roar. It could have been anyone's voice. The fact that I couldn't identify it would have worried me if there'd been time to think about it. But survival came first. I began to scramble towards one of the relatively intact structures. Ciara unclasped her hands from behind her head and followed me, perhaps because I was the only person she could clearly see through the haze. After all, we'd all heard stories of mistaking one of our own for the enemy when caught blind in close quarters. That mistake was almost always fatal. Those that lived wished they hadn't.

We kept crawling. The building might have been intentionally left standing so that my kind would take shelter there, thus letting the survivors get picked off as they regrouped. I didn't care about tactics. Being out in the open when the next sweep was made was certain death. Here, at least, was a chance for life. Solid concrete now stood between any possible repeat blasts and us. I asked between gasps, "Are you injured?"

"No."

"Same here." There was another variable EMP blast. Beams of white light materialized through the missing chinks in the wall. My pupils narrowed instantly to compensate, allowing me to see the harsh outlines that made the cramped space look like an old-fashioned black and white movie. The enemy didn't know about such old cultural icons. Culture was irrelevant to them. So was almost everything else we cared about. That's part of what made us the enemy to them. We were wasteful, soft, and irrelevant. We weren't meant to inherit the earth.

When the light and sound show faded, it seemed safe enough to comment. "The cyborgs really want to get rid of us." I laughed. We'd been thinking the same thing

"Yeah."

"Do you think many of our crèche-mates survived?" I wondered if others were in similar hiding places, thinking the same thing. As long as some of the bloodline survived, and remembered, the dead would still carry on through the living. My thoughts circled on those ideas, the central theme of the remembrance ceremony.

"Some of them had to," she whispered. We both wondered if she was right.

One glance from Ciara and I knew she agreed. We began to sneak back towards one of the entrances to the crèche, dodging from hiding place to hiding place. When it was in sight, I caught Cara's arm and pulled her back. "Wait!"

"What!"

"They had to have known where the crèche was to have attacked us so precisely. And they did so without any of the warning systems kicking in. They knew exactly where to strike, where our vulnerabilities were ... And they probably know our first instinct would be to go home and regroup with any other survivors."

"We can't wait out here."

"If we stay out here, we can see if anyone else comes back home. If we go in, we might walk into a trap."

"You think the enemy might already be inside?"

"Maybe."

Ciara finally understood. "All right. Let's wait to see if any cyborgs show up outside. If they do, then they aren't in yet.

If they're not in the crèche, then it will be evacuated to the secondary location."

"Can we make it there over land?"

"Is there a better option?"

"Why else stay out here?"

"If snipers are in place, they'll betray their presence by shooting at us. That might save others who don't know the level of danger." She paused a moment as we tried to get to a safer location that still showed a view of home. "Think any humans still survive?"

"Why do you ask?"

"We think more like them than the enemy does."

"They don't like us."

"We're not the ones who started the war."

"True, but humans sometimes blame all non-humans for the war."

"They're the ones that started killing us."

"Us? You're grouping our kind with tank-born, machine modified-?"

"I suppose our ancestor's biological manipulations, added DNA, and little extras make us utterly human?" I asked.

"We're not part machine."

"We were different enough for humans to kill our kind, too, when they started rounding up all of their descendants."

"And we killed a few back in self-defense."

"After they started sterilizing and brainwashing –"

"They lost billions. We lost thousands. The atrocities all evened out in the end. Or, at least, we're all about equal in numbers now."

"This discussion is not getting us anywhere."

"I'm just wondering that if we don't find our own kind, or can't make it back to the second location without drawing the enemy to our kin, can we try for safety with the humans?" Ciara asked.

I stared at her face for a long moment. What would humans think? Her high cheekbones and wide eyes gave her an elfin look. She did have a point. We looked like them on the surface. It was traits like the improved digestive tract, regenerative traits, higher intelligence, and rapid reflexes that set us apart. The rapid change in skin color and eye color in response to UV and lighting levels would reveal us the moment a doubting human threw a flashlight beam in our face. We would look human at first glance. If we got within visual range.

Maybe, once seen, we would be heard. Maybe. Would the little biological extras be seen as trivial now that the cyborgs had the upper hand? What's a third kidney compared to something with metal and plastic grafted on at birth? And weren't we all getting killed by the freaks?

"Maybe." Where was their last holdout in this area? It was a long way. They might - just might - take in a few of our kind. Assuming they, too, weren't hit in this strike. Assuming they still existed.

"There!" Ciara twisted to get a better view through a small opening as her body flattened to provide a smaller target. Elfin appearances could be deceiving. Our survival instincts were as hardwired as the cyborgs.

"A shadow."

"Where?"

"A rooftop. Can't tell which one." A pause. "Down!"

A beam of light lanced through the opening, striking Cara's shoulder as she tried to get out of the way. She screamed, slumped to the ground, unconscious. A portion of muscle and skin had been cut away. But the wound was cauterized by the weapon's blast and would not be fatal if the cyborgs didn't kill her. I waited long enough to be certain that the healing had begun. The cyborgs sometimes dumped bioweapons in the air to throw off the metabolism of our kind. Give us a slow death by injuries that would otherwise be modest. No wonder humans were disappearing faster than we were. I couldn't imagine how humans managed to survive as long as they had.

I saw a strike force enter the crèche. Alarms screamed this time. Sniper lasers swept through the fog. We couldn't go home, and we couldn't rejoin the group without risking them. Humans were the only hope. All I could do was buy enough time for Ciara to recover. If she found herself alone, she had a plan. I felt almost as alone as she would when she awoke.

I could see a sniper moving toward my position. I began a game of tag to get him away from Cara. We dodged after each other for what seemed like hours. The sniper came very close to getting me several times. My knife would only be of use up close, but we'd moved to battle scarred terrain, and the sniper no longer had a clear shot. Senses I'd never had to use became active. Sight and hearing sharpened. Smell grew and blossomed. I hated the creature for forcing me to hunt it, even as it hunted me.

The sniper was only visible in snatches; it was a blur driven by technological enhanced muscles, nerves, and brain. I kept ahead, just barely. Hadn't we been made as biological equivalent to the machine soldiers? The mutual chase led up to several stories above ground. Through corridors, around wreckage, across empty rooms it continued. Scenes from old horror movies flashed through my mind. The cyborg would have seen it as a weakness. Another weakness in the subspecies that had preferred sabotage and intrigue over hard combat. I was thinking like the enemy. I hated that mental comparison. Even as I knew it was ever so important to my survival.

Strategy. It was all I had. I couldn't let it know where I was going or what I was doing. If I acted like a distraction, it would backtrack to the mop up squad at the crèche. If I acted like I was running somewhere, it would extrapolate a direction, tell its friends my general direction, and pin me between two pincers while sweeping out in that direction. Strategy? The best thing to do was try to confuse the hell out of the machine. Maybe it would even relay bad data to its friends. Did those things really have friends?

I moved the chase back down to ground level. Hopefully, I'd given Ciara enough time to recover and run. Maybe I'd even pulled military strength from the crèche attackers and given others a chance to survive. Now it was time to focus on my own long-term survival. All I needed was – hopefully - an opening.

I saw it. An old battered heat shield wall. I looped around to leave a false heat trail and then climbed in. I hoped the infrared sensors tapped into its eyes wouldn't notice. I'd have a few moments at most before my body heat would radiate into the air and give me away.

I flattened against the wall, ready to turn the corner and continue the chase if need be, when I heard the sound. A faint whir. Did he let me hear it in hopes that revulsion would cause an instinctive gagging? I managed to control myself. Barely. It was nearby. Horror and disgust warred with fear. Death was close. Around the corner? There was a soft click. Yes, around the corner. Looking for me. It found me.

The knife was solid in my hand. I turned it, blade pointing inward. I ducked, sliced with the handle at what I knew was empty air, felt a hand turn the knife around, and struck. There was a clatter, and then a heavier thud. After a moment, I stepped around the corner. To step too soon might have risked a weapon blast to the torso. Too late would have only cost a hand. Unpleasant strategy, but perhaps a survivable one.

The knife had been thrust straight towards the body, but the cyborg had twisted sideways. It had gone at an angle, cut through light armor, and grazed into the flesh. The blade might have killed it if it had gone in straight and ruined an un-augmented organ, or broke a circuit or something like that. The cyborg was doubled over on the ground around the weapon, injured. But not mortally so. It was trying to slowly work the weapon out.

On an alien impulse, I rolled it onto its back. The plastic armor, breathing gear, and uniform revealed only a vaguely humanoid form. I grabbed its own knife and held it. Yeah, it was injured. I'd gotten the knife before it could stop me.

It might not have been able to stop me if I shoved the sharp blade under the chin and into the brain. We knew that route, at least, could still be fatal to them. I'd never killed before. Curiosity could be a fatal weakness. I pulled off its facemask.

Another filter mask covered the lower face. Tiny cybernetic interfaces on either side of the eyes were visible. The LEDs flashed in sync to an unknown song, talking to neural networks wrapped within that skull. Dark brown eyes stared back at me. Augmentation was only in the retina? Those could have been a human's eyes.

It waited for me to strike. No fear. No waiting for friends. Just waiting for me to get it over with. I couldn't do it. I'd expected featureless metallic globes to stare back. Or maybe I'd expected red snake eyes like creatures out of one's nightmares. Not eyes that could have belonged to a crèche mate. Not something as humanoid as I was. I got up and began to walk away. My shoulders set, my body braced for the blast sure to come. It still had its taser, and I was in range. Five meters. Ten meters. Twenty paces. Out of range. Unless it had gotten up. I didn't look back. I just started running.

It was torture to make my way back where I'd left Cara. She was barely conscious when I returned. "Is it dead?"

"Can you walk?"

"Think so." She staggered up. "I can't go fast enough for us to make it out alive. Let's go back to the crèche. Some medical supplies had to survive..."

"The crèche was taken."

"If it has been taken, then its been abandoned by now. The soldiers would have found it empty or killed everyone. They wouldn't expect us to go back now ..."

I couldn't disagree.

Inside the crèche was pure and utter wreckage, but no bodies. Because everyone had gotten away? Or because they'd been cleared out? I didn't want to think about it. I propped her in a doorway. "Stay here."

I tiptoed down corridors towards a rear supply room. The emotional loss of the place I'd known most of my life, and knowing that most of my kin were dead, slowed me down. Thinking of Cara, I sped up again. Down a side corridor, I found dead friends. I couldn't get where I was going. I started to backtrack and walked straight into a cyborg mop-up squad ensuring the dead were truly dead.

Several laser rifles were aimed at me. They conferred via occasional words and who knew what else. One in particular waved its rifle, indicating I should move. The others left the room and continued the sweep for the living. A second crew came through, taking the bodies for who knew what purpose.

My captor shoved me into an empty refuge room. My heart fell. This room was supposed to be able to withstand anything. Obviously, it hadn't. Was it going to kill me here to minimize the mess? Did it want something messier to satisfy emotions that kind wouldn't admit to having? Or did it just like the irony of killing me in one of the safest corners in the crèche?

It mechanically scanned the hall in both directions for a while. I had no exit but past the thing, and had no way to get past it. The hall seemed empty. It then took two paces inside the room and closed one of the outer doors. The laser rifle aimed straight at my heart. Then the cyborg moved it up and sideways by a few degrees and fired twice. The wall just behind me was badly scorched.

The cyborg reached a hand up to its outer mask. It methodically undid the seals. It removed the mask, revealed dark brown eyes for a few seconds, and then put the mask back on. It turned and walked out the doorway. It closed the door again. Then it fired. The door was welded shut by the blast.

I was trapped. I tried my knife against the weld. I was still working on it when a vicious multi-frequency EMP blast set the door aglow. Only the thick walls of this inner sanctum protected me. The laser sealed door held well enough to keep the air, heated by microwave radiation out, from cooking me. As the blast faded, the door fell off the hinges. The burst had destroyed anything that might possibly have survived the cyborg assault. Even the walls had begun to crumble around me. If I hadn't been so deep underground with the reinforced door, I would have certainly been killed.

Ciara was not where I had left her. No dead body. No charred residue. Nor was anything of her anywhere to be found. Was she captured? Dead? Wandering delirious on the surface? Found by our own kind and evacuated? I knew the last thought was unlikely, but it was a thought to hold on to. There was nothing else for me to hold on to of my former life.

Where now? Where had my crèche-mates gone? I couldn't go to rendezvous site. It was too likely I'd be followed. Towards the last place I knew humans might be? That, too, might kill them if I were followed. The mop up squads knew they sometimes missed a few.

I picked a direction at random and began to walk. I'd find someone, somewhere. If cyborgs could be part human, part of the time, then we weren't all utterly and completely different. If there was that in common, then we all had a chance. I knew the last thought was unlikely, but it was a possibility to hold onto. Thin red rays of sunlight made it through the clearing haze. I couldn't tell if it was sunrise or sunset. But it was light to walk by, so I was grateful.

CATHEDRAL

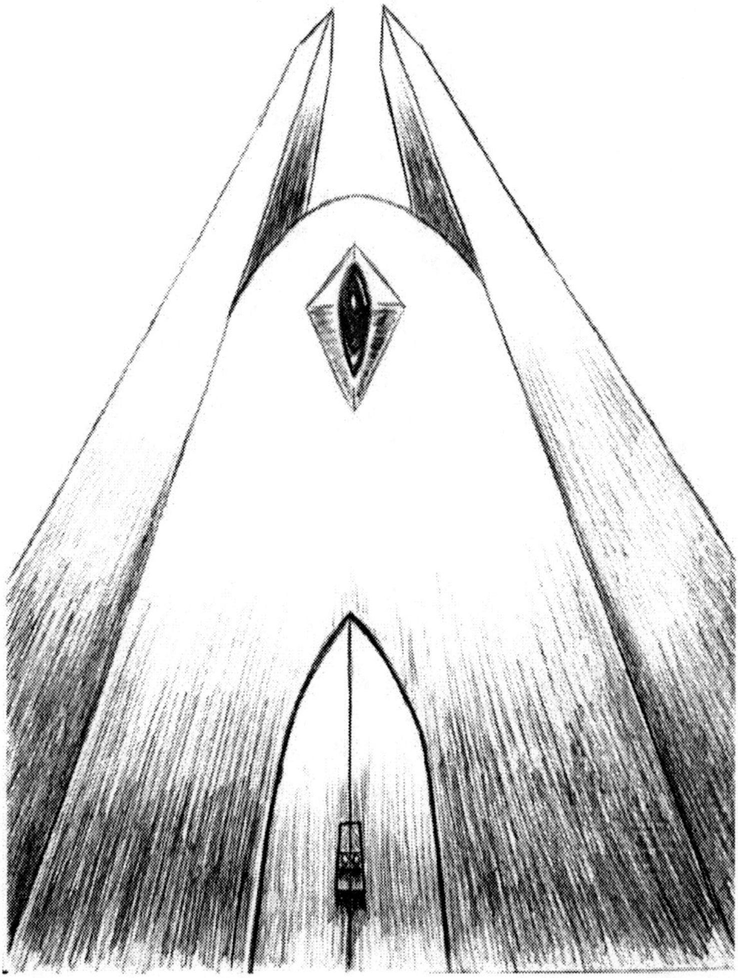

Even genetically engineered geniuses have their problems . . .

CATHEDRAL

Loud music thundered on over the murmurs of conversations. The off-duty crowd flowed past the bar. The drink in my hand was refilled every time the waiter came near. Last week, I would have been careful not to have too much caffeine. The buzz it created for my kind was almost a great as normal people got off alcohol. Not long ago, I would not have risked the image of a caffeine addict. Now I did not care about image or the cost of the drinks. My stipend would last far longer than I would.

The flow of humanity had once been a comforting sight to me. Here was what we had been working for. Here was our reason for existing. Here were the people we were here to help. Now the sight of them was depressing. The least of them would usually live much longer than I would. Yet I watched them go by for lack of anything better to do.

I turned my attention to the human now beside me. "Anything else, miss?" It was a different waiter. The previous waiter had disappeared. He was likely looking for normal customers. The sugar was getting to me, so I decided on a more civilized beverage. "Hot tea, please."

"Your credit chit, miss?" He glanced at it before blanching for a moment. He recognized the government account number and knew what it meant. The man composed himself and left. He brought back a full pitcher. "I hope this will suffice for the rest of your stay here?" I nodded. He charged the account and then went on in his rounds. He was glad to no longer have to deal with my kind. I tried to focus on the music to distract me from the chaos around me.

The music suddenly grew louder. The world swam before my eyes for a split second. My left hand tensed into a fist. Would it begin trembling? Would the random memory flashes begin, a symptom of the nervous system failure that would eventually kill me? How long after the memory flashes would the hallucinations drown out reality? How long after that would it be before the coma claimed me? Just as abruptly, it was over.

We're supposed to be smart. Genetically engineered geniuses, designed to solve all of the world's problems, so the average people don't have to bother with such concerns as curing cancer and preventing plagues. The first of my kind were found to have minds that ran so fast that a few years after adulthood, the neurochemistry began producing toxic byproduct faster than the liver could break them down. The enhanced livers and kidneys of the next generation increased our lifespan by a few years.

Most of us lived to age 25. All were dead by 30. Our creators didn't care. If we died early in exchange for the brilliance we brought to the table, then it was considered a fair price.

Raised for a few years by foster parents, then educated in a controlled environment, and then put to work. Most of us didn't find out about the preprogrammed death sentence until the blade began falling. By then, it was too late to worry about the life we'd lived. Only a few seconds had elapsed as all of this ran through my mind. Then the world slowed down to proper pace. No one had noticed my lapse. In that brief time, I had been lost to the outside world.

I don't belong here, not with them. But where could I go? Yeren and Seru-che were dead. Berisca was comatose as of yesterday…Dannon? He had been discharged only a month ago. I checked a reference file on my wrist computer. According to the map, he lived nearby...People were beginning to notice the computer. Most of those here did not have the clearance for one. They only had access to a bulky terminal at home or work. One more bit of social engineering on the "outside." I could lapse again at any moment. I swore silently while leaving the room, moving with a grace acquired from years of intense physical training. They were not going to get the pleasure of seeing one of us for what they made us to be.

Thrust, parry, block. Dodge. Begin again. We moved with a speed humans could not achieve, striving for perfection in action even as our bodies failed. The rattle of dulled rapiers echoed through the room in a more regular pattern than our steps. "How long… have you… been out?" Dannon got out between breaths.

"A week."

"Am. I. Slowing?"

"A little." Honesty was programmed in to us, perhaps as much genetic as social engineering.

Dannon stopped suddenly, bowed, and began toweling off. "I want you to see something." He sat down heavily into a chair and called up a file on a palm-sized unit. The authorities would reclaim the machine the moment he was declared dead. It was a luxury we were afforded at this point in our lives. Release into the outside world was meant to be a mercy. It gave us a few months to taste the life everyone else enjoyed. Or so I was told when shown the door. In reality, our masters believed that those still working would cease being productive if they had to watch the decline of those near death.

I'd realized it was another social manipulation of the mundane. We were myths to the average people. They saw us only near the end, when we were sick and failing. Seeing us this way and only this way made us pitiable. The pity countered the instinctive fear about the engineered advantages we had. It allowed the authorities to continue making us without the mundanes revolting.

"What is it?"

"A list of songs I've been listening to lately. If you want anything..." He noticed that his left hand was trembling. He tried to stop it and couldn't. "Smarter, faster, loyal and dutiful, and then—this!" He threw the device hard enough for it to strike the wall in his frustration. Dannon grimaced, realizing his emotional outburst. "I can't stand this. Not the anger, not the frustration, not the deterioration of emotional control. We never let emotions get in the way of work. Work, work, work. Just get as much done as possible - How old are you, Kat?"

"Twenty-five. And a half."

"I'm twenty-six.."

"Kihemek saw thirty." I used a gesture to ask, "Are others listening?"

Dannon said out loud, "I know how to disable them."

"Good. Continue."

"He suffered from those injections he'd concocted to extend his lifespan. You know our genetic code mutates radically if exposed to any effort to change it. That was a programmed-in control to prevent tampering. He was a geneticist; Kat, he knew better."

"He had a better chance at succeeding than the rest of us."

"He would have started sooner if he'd known he'd been born with a death sentence."

"We all learned at an early age we weren't…normal."

"Did you know at that early age you would die young?"

"Not specifically."

"What did they tell you?"

"All the lines they were supposed to use."

"Were you told what you were by your foster parents or by the Proctors that you were," he lapsed into silence as he contemplated the word he would use, "…different?"

"Parents."

"How did they handle having you taken away by the Proctors?"

"They knew what to expect. I was the fourth one they'd taken care of."

"My foster parents treated me like a human child. I was four years old. I had no idea why it was happening." Dannon went white for a moment, eyes glazed and seeing through and beyond me. He was looking back on the day he was taken away and taken "home", but it was clear he'd been close to fear when it happened. Then he was back with me. "Sorry. Memories."

A flush crept into his cheeks at embarrassment that he'd drifted away from reality. It was an alien reaction by one of our kind. The emotional storms that wracked the mundane were mere breezes for us until the breakdown started. Until we were staring death in the face. It was an irony that our creators never bothered to solve. Gut-wrenching fear wasn't possible until the time we were most likely to experience it. Obeying some foreign impulse, I moved to his side. He tensed at my hand on his arm.

Hours together on the gym floor, being stationed together on the same projects over the years, and never had either of us talked to anyone this way. Too busy, maybe. Was that another reason we were driven to work so hard, so we didn't think about anything else? But what else was there to think about? Each other? "Are we friends, Dannon?"

"I suppose."

We sat in awkward silence for a long time. Finally, I decided to break it. "Send me messages, if you want." He did not answer. His mind had gone back to his childhood, the time before the Proctors came. I stepped away from him; it was disquieting to see. Yet he didn't seem upset. The bad emotions would come when memories of the Proctors came back to him. I stared at the room around me in an effort to get my mind off of his mind.

His apartment was large and mostly empty. We had all been raised with the luxury of wide-open space around us. In a world of nine billion people, it was a luxury most would have screamed about if they knew. This place was a single man's mark on the universe, his private space. A desk and a shelf stacked with memory crystals, a bare kitchen with a few boxes of rations, a futon for sleep that came more than it should have, and the practice mat we'd used. No personal belongings except for the music collection and the computer. And the computer was something on loan.

Everything here could be cleared out within moments of his death, leaving no trace he had ever been here. The implant put in all of us within minutes of birth would send out the signal within minutes of death so that our bodies could be retrieved. The apartment would be empty again, swept utterly clean for the next anonymous and unknown occupant. It might even be one of our kind left to repeat the whole process over again.

Nothing left except the data we had created in our productive years. If the data of our last days was interesting, we might be dissected. Otherwise, it was on to cremation. One more bit of data before we ceased to exist in any form. I shivered violently at the thought of what lay ahead. Yet my own decline had barely begun.

It shouldn't have to be this way. "Dannon, goodbye." He didn't respond to my leaving. He was still caught up in his mental lapse. A chill hit me amidst a kaleidoscope of thoughts: Kihemek's work when he'd focused on extending his own survival. I was a biochemist. He had told me how to do what he wanted done.

Here, now, I could still act.

A year ago, this behavior would have been unthinkable. Now? Well, times change. So do people, especially when they face the Long Night. The basement had been an illegal drug factory. Kihemek had reported them to authorities. He discovered the facility shortly after his release. He took over the remaining equipment and stock and moved it to a new location. Now it was mine. In some ways, the return to work was comforting. It was a distraction to the mental chaos that seemed to hover in the shadows, waiting for me.

I had no desire to try to contact those still living out the life I'd once had, as Kihemek had felt the need to do. The communications he'd sent to a few of us inside that he thought would agree with him would have gotten us in trouble if discovered. We were unable to reply, but we knew the location of the facility. It was a chance. No more, no less. There was no sign those that had preceded me had chosen to follow in his footsteps. They had either become resigned to their fate or were too afraid to act.

Kihemek had left his notes on paper. He didn't want a random crowd-control EMP blast to destroy his work. He'd promised an extended life span–"interminable" was the exact word. That was the promise that had brought me here. The hypospray hissed softly as the engineered enzymes entered my bloodstream. When awake I was always in peak condition. But when it came time to use the counter-agent to sleep, the symptoms caught up with a vengeance.

I screamed after reading his notes. Interminable had been his word; he meant "eternal." He'd managed to improve the quality of life, but not its length. Kihemek discovered that he had been an anomaly. If he'd been mundane, he would have lived 120 years or more. He was just long-lived. There would be no extra years of life. All of those hopes were dead. As dead as we would all be, even after following his false promises.

It was worse than phony promises. He'd found religion out here. He meant eternal as in an afterlife. It was sheer insanity. When I first read his work, I decided he'd simply gone over the deep end in one fell swoop, rather than the normal slow deterioration. He thought he'd live forever. In one way or another. Crazy.

Not all of it was craziness. In some ways, he was right. *Morality for us had always been finding the Truth*, Kihemek wrote on one note. Truth for us had always involved solving the problems placed in front of us. Out here he'd discovered that we'd been creating more problems for the outside world than we'd solved. On that much I could agree with him.

Cultures were turning out my prize-winning work (prize winning in the unlikely event the rest of the world ever found out). The nanotech processors (used to keep track of me) required minimal supervision, but it was time to go somewhere else. I could not stay too long and risk drawing undue attention to this location.

Spires reaching for the great blue above rivaled the city skyline from this angle. I stepped over and around the addicts on the concrete as I walked towards them. Kihemek had found a way to turn off the implants. I went to the cathedrals in the morning, turned off the implant, and then went to work. I went back in the evening and turned the implant back on. As far as any tracker was concerned, I'd been there all day.

No witnesses would ever say I had or had not been there. They would have to admit that they'd been there as well, and no one wanted to admit to a government official that they'd been associated with religion. It wasn't illegal, *yet*, but it could make one's life more difficult than it already was.

No one paid attention to me sitting in the back row. Those here were mostly old or infirm, those individuals society had written off and paid no heed to. In that regard, I was like them. The daily choir music of tired voices and the stained glass patterns were new to me. They were a delight to the eye. If I lapsed while staring at them, no one thought to interrupt me. If I was conscious, it didn't matter if my vision blurred. I could appreciate the music and the delicate shades of lighting. They were a pretty sight in a bland, gray world.

"Not many people your age come here these days." I turned to see—a deacon?—standing beside me. "You've been here every service for a week." He held out a hand to me. "Father Daniels."

"Katarina Lee-Delanoirre." He seemed... compassionate? Caring? The words had never been part of my vocabulary before. He was very different from anyone else I had ever known. He radiated a sense of purpose. For a moment, I envied him. Then I remembered how much more difficult his life must be for the job he held. The harassment, the questionings, the constant monitoring. Monitoring. I was being watched. The last thought brought me fully back to myself.

"What do you do?"

Would it hurt to be honest with him? What would the authorities do? Round us both up again? "I was a biochemist with a pharmaceutical company."

"Were you laid-off?"

"No." His concerned expression begged for more of an answer. "I'm retired."

Confusion flitted across his face for a moment before the realization came. He recognized my genotype now. The geneticists threw in a little variety so we didn't all look alike; they were only partially successful. He knew what I was now. At least there was no revulsion like the other churches when they realized what I was. "They prefer pure technology, the museums or libraries, not churches," he murmured to himself. To me directly he asked, "What did you do?"

"Research and development."

He knew there was only one kind of pharmaceutical research going on these days. The Father became angry. "Did you know you were creating new addicts?"

"Does it matter?"

"That was not an answer to my question."

"I was told it was for the sick." I had been told it was for control of the mentally unstable. What I didn't know at that time was that every person on the street fell into that category. No one was happy anymore unless injected. Many wanted to escape. For some, it was staring at the stain glass windows. For others, it was into a hallucinagenic fog.

The Father was choosing to escape from the "uncomfortable" in his own way. We were walking toward the doors. Father Daniels escorting me out. Politely, but out. "My purpose is to work towards the benefit of the majority." Pure rhetoric, but I thought it had been true at the time. At least it was true now.

"Can you swear to it?" His challenge was a tired one. He expected an indignant argument by which he could slam the door closed and put an end to my presence in his refuge. At least he wasn't cursing me, calling me a soulless creation in a human's image. I hated it when they called me such things. I'd created things, too, in my life. That required a mind in the very least, if not a soul as well. "I wish that were possible."

"It's too late to do anything about how your work was used."

No, it wasn't too late, but I couldn't tell him that. I merely nodded and left. The thick wooden doors of this sanctuary were closed to me as others had been before.

Dannon had let me move in and take care of him before the end. He didn't notice my absences. He scarcely noticed my presence.

Picking up the few items he needed, but could no longer get, had seemed the right thing to do. But now he was gone, and he wasn't coming back. I wanted to curse the tracking implant imbedded at the base of my skull. If I tried to remove it, it would kill me. At best, it could be turned off to allow a little privacy. I hated it, just as I hated the inevitable. I hated Dannon's loss. Seeing Dannon gone, I'd fallen to the floor and cried. Irrational, but I could no longer control my emotions. Was it better that he wasn't here and unable to see me this way?

The weight of the emotional overload was pulling me down. I wanted to sleep, to dream, to let the memories come. The emptiness of the huge space around me was too much to bear alone. Images tumbled through my mind –

- Jumping on the bed, the quilts in a pile on the floor, my two stuffed animals watching from the dresser, as I tried to get higher. Jared came in, still wearing his doctor's outfit, "You should be studying, Kat," and he caught me in mid-air. "You know better than to waste your time at play -

- "Katarina, you won't ever see us again," Argentine said as the Proctors came to take me away from her and Jared, to take me back to where they said I belonged, where they said I should want to be, with others like me. Jared waved a small wave. "You'll learn all sorts of new things we can't teach you." His voice cracked on the line I later learned came straight out of the "Successful Separation" chapter of their manual –

- "Maintain your stance!" The instructor shouted, karate students obeyed, not minding the discipline and enjoying the exercise. It was a chance to work the body as hard as the mind worked the rest of the day. Discipline, always there was discipline. Freedom was chaos, and chaos was unnatural, or so the lecture went, and on the lesson went -

- Seeing an addict for the first time on the street, as I headed to Kihemek's lab for the first time, asking for money to buy a compound I had developed -

-Father Daniels saying it was too late to do anything, the unaccustomed pain, knowing that he was condemning me for my work, not just for being what I was-

- The unabashed revulsion of locals seeing me on a street corner, as I faded in and out of reality. Staring, uncertain if I was an addict, like those I had supplied, or an unnatural creature that was only tolerated as for the critical role I played in the world. They were all glad they were not me -

- Dannon rambling on about his foster parents, me sitting there, wishing he would finish or stop, feeling more alone with every word -

Wave after wave, the memories growing more intense as my life was relived moment for moment. The artificial enzymes helped hold back the deterioration, but no longer. I cried tears at memories that I had never realized had been painful. I couldn't change the past. No matter. Soon, the damage I'd caused would be undone.

"And for the other news, the latest drug to hit the streets: 'Cathedral', hit the top of the market because of the rush it gave without any obvious side-effects. Furthermore, those who used it note a blurring of vision into a soft glow of color reminiscent of stain-glass windows. After several doses of 'Cathedral,' however, it is impossible to experience any pleasant effects from alcohol or any standard issue intoxicants, including Cathedral itself. Doctors have determined that the effect is permanent. However, given the cheapness and easy availability of the drug, millions have already taken it. It is not known to authorities what group created Cathedral..."

The news broadcast was one of the last bits of the outside world that reached me. There are only the memories now. I did what I was meant to do.

I kept the promise you wanted me to make, Father Daniels. I can see the colors coming through the cathedral windows in the sunlight. The colors are beautiful this time in the morning. Can't you see it? Can anyone else see it?

Dannon, where are you? Don't you want to talk to me? I'll listen to the stories of your foster parents now. Dannon?

Where am I?

I'm falling. I'm falling onto the bed. I'm jumping back up. Jared, Argentine, you don't like me jumping on the bed. I can't go any higher than this. Jared, Argentine! Are you going to catch me? I'm falling!

... And no one's there to catch me...

DENNY

Beware of the Bum.

DENNY

"Hey, you! Get out of there!"

Denny slowly raised his head and looked at the shopkeeper impassively. He'd been spoken to, and some instinct said to look up. Then, without further thought, he went back to rummaging through the garbage. Denny did not notice the shopkeeper again until he was practically breathing down Denny's neck. Only the close proximity of another took any attention from his search.

"Get a job, you bum." The shopkeeper grew angrier at Denny's silence.

Sick and tired of the street life driving away his customers, he let it all loose. "I'll bet you leech off the system, right? You'll never work. You won't change." Denny was barely aware of the dull drone in the background. The shopkeeper, upset that he didn't have the likely drunk lowlife's attention, drummed up the rhythm, "Beggar! Tramp! Vagrant! Low-life! Look at me when I talk to you -" The shopkeeper grabbed Denny's shoulder in order to whirl him about.

Denny's awareness exploded at the moment of physical contact. Denny awoke from the perpetual dreaming he was caught in since the accident at the physics lab. He heard the screams as the fiery energy burst out from the physical contact. Whether he had crossed a quantum reality threshold or was simply out of sync with the rest of the universe, contact with anyone - anything at all living - was fatal. He desperately wanted answers; without answers, there could be no help. Without help, this torment would never end.

Denny looked down and saw the dead body sprawled across the pavement. Denny realized what had happened and howled, in anguish, in guilt, in despair, in denial. It had happened again!

In the dreaming state, when the energy he'd picked up from the experiment overwhelmed his brain, he was essentially unaware of the world, running on automatic. Those few moments he was fully aware and in sync with reality, only existed when someone or something died as the energy or physical interaction brought him fully to himself. He could not completely understand, because he could never remain awake and aware long enough to think things through. Maybe, just maybe, he'd find something he could touch or hold or use that would take the energy away, letting him live without ending lives.

Denny's howl was cut short within moments. Numbness flooded in as the energy discharge faded, and with it, full awareness. It wasn't another social worker or charitable giver. The man had been a jerk. The emotional chaos caused by the death made the return to dullness almost welcome. His life wasn't important; his death certainly wasn't important. The search. He had to continue the search.

Denny shuffled over to the next dumpster, not really certain what he was looking for. His feet were dragging on the ground with a growing sense of weight. His body was beginning to slump from many kinds of fatigue. The need to keep looking, to find something – he wasn't sure what – took over again.

GONE IN A FLASH

Can suicide be a valid life choice?

GONE IN A FLASH

"What did you do today?" My grandson was quiet, but not as morose as usual. It was an improvement over his usual state. "Well?"

"I went to the park," he finally admitted. "I saw a Lightshow."

I dropped the plate in my hands. The shattering of the antique ceramic meant nothing in that moment. "Who?"

"I don't know."

"You saw someone die, and you don't know who?"

"I don't know. It just happened."

"It just happened?"

"The guy committed suicide. It happens."

"You know that suicide is wrong."

"I thought you let Grandpa die a natural death."

"That's different."

"You chose not to continue his life."

"He died a natural death. We didn't use artificial means of prolonging his life."

"He ended it how he chose to."

Choice. You either chose to fight tooth and nail to keep you going for 150 years or you ended it in a flash. "Was the suicide a protestor?"

"He didn't have any signs up or anything."

"Was there a crowd of friends or family?"

"No."

"Why would someone commit suicide in public and not even make a public statement?" I knew people often chose to "go" in a pretty place like Regan Park. They should do it at home or in a hospital – anywhere but where people like me might see it.

"The Phoenix were handing out Flashers. The guy just took one and did it."

"In public?"

"Yeah."

"The police didn't stop them?"

"They had a hazmat team nearby in case something went wrong."

"And someone walked up and committed suicide like that?" I snapped my fingers.

"Pretty much."

"I'm glad you left. It's getting insane."

"Yeah. Some old fogy was yelling that they couldn't do that sort of thing."

"Good. Suicide is wrong. Suicide in public is worse."

"No. He was complaining that all these people killing themselves meant nobody would pay into the retirement system."

"That system is broke anyway."

"A Phoenix said it didn't matter what age a person was. One of the women said the old guy probably killed some of his own kids before they were born, or even afterward if they didn't meet spec. Or he'd have denied them medical treatment and let them die – and that's murder if it isn't suicide. So if we can all die at any age for anyone else's reason, why not at our own time for our own reason?"

He'd listened. He'd paid attention. Their words and reasoning was sinking in to his impressionable mind. "Jacob, do you know why suicide is wrong?"

"You said that life is precious."

"What else?"

"Don't go into the God stuff."

God stuff. Right and wrong, good and evil, it was all God stuff. Off limits stuff. "You can't get your life back once you make *that* mistake. You can't undo *that* mistake. You can't come back from the dead."

"What about reincarnation?"

"Unless a squirrel comes up to me and says, 'Hi, I was your cousin Chandra before she got killed in the Times Square Tragedy,' I won't believe that clap trap."

"It's cleaner than all the others ways you can go."

Flashers were popular because of all the things it wasn't. It wasn't painful, just a half second high heat explosion. It wasn't messy; it left a faint burn marks and some ashes. It didn't kill innocent people if you were at least 10 meters away from anyone else, so there was no guilt.

Since the terrorists had devised the horrific devices - and they'd been mass-produced before we won the Jihad – they were common. A small shiny thing that fit in your hand. Press the code, and you go up in a flash of fiery light. No mess, no fuss. The fact that the light was pure white led many with no spirituality to relate it to enlightenment. Suicide was becoming an impulse act with no consequences except your death.

"Why aren't the cops stopping it? Those Flashers are dangerous."

"That's why they were there. So that no one who didn't want to die didn't."

"So no one who doesn't want to die does?" I corrected.

"They're supposed to protect lives."

"Then they should have stopped the Phoenix –"

"But it's an individual's choice! It's their right! –"

"It's their life!"

"Why should somebody with no hope stick around? Aside from taking care of old farts and paying taxes for everyone else? Or -"

"To have their own families one day."

"Or blindly continue the bloodline so their elders can have their genetic immortality? Who's being selfish now?"

I felt a knot in my stomach then, a cold tightness that wouldn't let go. I knew the feeling from when I'd lost my husband. Grief for those still living, but about to be lost. "I love you."

"I know."

"You need to spend time with the living. Your cousins-perhaps."

"You raised those girls up to be breeders."

Dismissive. Full of contempt. People who valued life tended to carry it on with full enthusiasm. My two granddaughters had already had three children between them. My grandson, unfortunately, never saw the point.

"They made *their* choice."

I couldn't stand this discussion. Not from my own kin, my own flesh and blood. I'd lost my husband and children in the war against the Muslims and their cult of death. I'd raised their children as my own, trying my best. I was failing to get through to the only male left in the family. "If you don't want to listen to me, why don't you just leave?"

"I will." The knot in my stomach got tighter. This is why he was so calm. In fact, it was likely why he'd come by in the first place. He then casually whipped an invitation out of his pocket. "Don't worry. I'm not impulsive. I still care about everybody. That's why I didn't do it today. Next Saturday. Will you be there?"

KYOTO PLUS TEN

All that work for a burger . . .

KYOTO PLUS TEN

Jordan flipped the burgers every few seconds, whether they needed it or not. The barbeque was an act of bliss. A siren shrieked in the distance. Jordan scrunched down to avoid being seen. Then he closed the grill's lid, burning his fingers as it slammed down. "Damn, Kyoto", he muttered.

He had a permit for the meat, but not for the barbeque. The illegal carbon emission charge couldn't be bought off with a steak the way he'd kept from getting ticketed when he had illegally acquired meat.

The sirens grew distant. It wasn't in his direction. Jordan came up a few centimeters. He'd picked this alley close to the industrial section in the hopes that the carbon dioxide would be blamed on mechanical causes. Standing in the alley, with the grill hidden behind a trashcan, was the safest way he could think of cooking this way. This was the first beef he'd had in six months, and he wanted to cook it the way his father had. A microwave just wasn't good enough. Nor was it truly safe, with the regular blackouts. Blackouts could render him unable to cook the meat before it went bad, or microwave could leave the meat undercooked.

Russians didn't have problems like this. Their economy had been collapsing before they had ratified the Kyoto Treaty. Their declining population gave them an abundance of carbon credits per capita. They had *bonfires* in the old Soviet squares at Solstice.

But could Americans do that? *Nooooo* ... Americans were rich, evil industrialists who'd polluted the world too much to be allowed even simple joys like an occasional cooking by real fire. There might be more barbeque permits for people like him if they persecuted homeless people with open fires to keep warm. Or he'd get one if he lived long and got very rich … but the 60% income tax, meant to pay for the baby boomer retirees' benefits and the unemployment checks, made it but a faint dream. That's why he had to enjoy his beef ration from the culled dairy herds in secret. It was far better than the illegally acquired cat meat the homeless often sold to buy rationed vegetables trucked in from afar.

Jordan stood back up. He flipped back the grill's lid. Nothing was burned. It smelled good. Much better than the tofu and krill cakes his friends claimed were acceptable substitutes. Jordan shifted to look like he was scavenging in the trashcans as some pedestrians cut through the nearly-empty wing of the industrial complex. Then they stopped near a door. The security guards came outside and quizzed everyone for a long time. After bribes were taken, the pedestrians pulled out attaché cases and resumes.

He tried not to curse to himself. He hadn't known there was anyone hiring out here! The first come first serve people would have been tipped off in advance and be allowed in. But word of interviews would start a long line by 6 AM!

Jordan started cursing the Goddess as he started dousing the fire with dirt. The meat was close to done. Was it safe to transport? He didn't have a choice. He started looking around furtively. Neither guard had seemed to take notice of him, as they stood outside the hiring office. Nor had other applicants started arriving.

He despondently left the meat in the grill as he closed it up. It would get dirty, but this was the only chance he had of being able to save it for later. Jordan had hoped to eat it here to eliminate any evidence of his crime. He'd even hoped to abandon the grill in a metal recycling hopper so that he'd walk away scotch free with a stomach full. No one would question a man who claimed to add so many pounds of metal to the recycling effort, and any fingerprints would have disappeared with the 7AM roundup and meltdown.

Jordan slung the grill over his shoulder by his makeshift strap. He started grabbing some scrap rusty steel sections to carry to keep his precious cargo out of sight. Hopefully, he could carry it all to a recycling bin near his apartment. From there, he hoped to make it into his efficiency, before anyone who knew him saw enough to be suspicious of him suddenly taking up recycling without threats from the Community Board.

CLOSING NOTES

After reading the author's manuscript I saw a theme in these stories: Random acts of survival. Reading these stories made me wonder if that was what our existence equates to? Are we simply here to survive and perpetuate the species?

However, there are a number of acts of kindness in this book, which gives me hope in us as a species. For we are one people no matter what Al Qaeda or the Neo Nazis might say. Hopefully, this book will motivate some of its readers to look past their own pursuit of survival, and do something for the betterment and furthering of all humanity.

ABOUT THE AUTHOR

Tamara Wilhite is a degreed engineer, professional technical writer, a freelance fiction writer, and mother of 2 young children. Mrs. Wilhite's work has been featured in a number of publications including: IIE, Spaceflight, CQ, and Woman Engineer.

ABOUT THE ILLUSTRATOR

Robert Holsonbake is a Freelance Graphic Artist that resides in Plano, Texas. He has been drawing since the age of seven and got into computer graphics when he started high school. His education came from the Art Institute of Dallas for 3D animation and Visual Effects.

Robert started doing freelance work in 2001, mainly from word of mouth and still uses that method to this day. The work that he does consists of illustrations, photo manipulation, web sites, logos, print ads, video, and of course 3D animation and visual effects.

Robert was born on June 15th, 1978 in Purcell, Oklahoma. He grew up and graduated there, then decided to further his education in Dallas, Texas in 1998. He is very passionate about his work and believes that he will be doing art for the rest of his life.

Printed in the United States
99434LV00001B/77/A